MW01167442

OSA

© 2021 Copyright David Lady
ISBN: 9798709423350

Imprint: Independently published, Ocala Florida USA

All rights reserved. No part of these publications
may be reproduced, distributed, or transmitted in
any form or by any means, including photocopying,
recording, or other electronic or mechanical
methods, without the prior written permission of
the publisher, except in the case of brief quotations
embodied in critical reviews and certain other
noncommercial uses permitted by copyright law.

This is a work of fiction. Any resemblance
to actual events or persons, living or
dead, is entirely coincidental.

DAVID EDWARD

"It is never what you think it is but always what was agreed." - Judge Stone

DAVID EDWARD

Alamosa

The shadows are the smalls. The between. They are brought about by the little acts. The little sins. Not the big ones. Sometimes justice and the law differ because of them.

At least that is the theory offered by Judge Stone in the 1870's post-civil war Colorado Territory. Being a federal judge and deciding the law often present conflicting problems. Nothing is easy. Clear choices are hard to come by.

When the murder trial of a Denver City lawyer in the town of Alamosa erupts in violence, it ignites a series of events that could endanger not just the people of Colorado but be the powder keg starting a second civil war between east and west. A vast conspiracy exposed in both this world and the next.

It all hinges on the guilt or innocence of one woman. But she is already dead.

Set in the richly described post-civil war America, Alamosa is a thought-provoking western adventure. It is both a classic western and an anti-western. Calling into question many norms of the genre and providing clever insight into the human condition: what it means to bring justice, and how justice by itself might not be enough.

DAVID EDWARD

1875 - Summer

DAVID EDWARD

PROLOG

The town of Alamosa reeked like the north end of a southbound mule.

The sun burned hot and bright in the cloudless sky.

A small lake nearby was bluer than blue. The fields in the valley were dark green and lush. There were yellow and purple flowers in the fields and the very top of the mountain peaks in the distance were still white with snow.

The cool overnight mountain air had given up. It did every day about this time. Losing its daily battle to the relentless energy of the summer sun.

Waves of heat fell hard coming in at angles to the horizon. Having defeated the night air the sun was now working on everything else. The town and the landscape glowed white on the edges because of it. The higher elevations putting everything that much closer.

In town everything was hot. The sun baked things like the inside of an expensive city slicker oven. You could see the heat bounding here and there just having a grand old time.

Alamosa's Courthouse stood grand and intimidating under it all in the center of town against the majestic backdrop. The building was built by the locals as a hopeless bid to be the territory capital in anticipation of Colorado becoming a state.

If you looked past the building and up into the mountains or looked over to the bright blue lake or looked north to the green flowered pastures, you wanted to go there instead of staying here.

You felt drawn away. A yearning. A desperate excuse to leave this hard luck crossroads town for any reason you could invent.

Here it was hot.

Here everything was hard. Even breathing was hard.

Once making a deliberate choice to inhale the hot oily air you immediately regret your decision. Forced to deal with the hypocrisy of the palpable stench in direct contrast to the picturesque surroundings.

Despite the ungodly temperature and mother nature's tempting distractions the town of Alamosa should be bustling this time of day. Instead, everyone was packing into the courthouse building for the scandalous end of the murder trial.

As the last of the townspeople pushed their way through the entryway, past the small clerk's office, and into the large courtroom, the bailiff said loudly "Please be seated".

The inside of the building was just as grand and intimidating as its exterior. It was cool and smelled different than the outside. Not better, the crowd of sweaty people brought in their own stink.

Still, the exterior stench willed its way in too. Managing to fill the courtroom with a palpable stench of dread. The oily stillness seeping here and there in the large room as if it had a mind of its own.

It searched for something. Someone maybe. Looking for more of its kind. Attracted to the muffled sobs of a plain looking young woman seated near the front. Whatever the hell it was it recoiled when it neared the man seated in the judge's chair. Judge Isaac Hobart Stone. Of sturdy build with piercing gray eyes, black hair, and a well-trimmed white beard.

He looked like a Judge from the picture books. The whole place did.

Stone could see the evil as it danced around the room. He hated at it and it hated right back.

A lone figure was seated at the defendant's table. James McGuire. A disheveled fat city lawyer who was providing his own defense for the charge of murder.

As everyone settled down McGuire rose from his chair. He wore a wrinkled white suit that showed stains at the armpit and around the collar. He held a dirty handkerchief to his nose and mouth. The evil stench paid it no mind and clung to him anyway. An ally from which it could taunt Stone.

Almost as if performing a magic trick McGuire nimbly used his hand to pocket the handkerchief he had been holding. It was a quick move. On casual observation the dirty cloth seemed to just vanish while he wiped his sweaty upper lip on the opposite sleeve of his well-worn suit before he spoke.

"If it pleases the court. I renew my objection to the perjured testimony of Maggie Summers," the fat man announced. He proudly looked about the room as a showman might with suddenly the handkerchief back in his opposite hand.

Stone stared at McGuire without blinking for a few moments. They finally locked eyes. Without a motion Stone looked to where Maggie Summers sat a few benches back from the front. Her face was puffy red. Snot ran down from her nose. The front of her blue dress was soaking wet with tears.

Turning his gaze to the center of the room with still little movement, Stone asked pleasantly, "Has anyone seen Sheriff Burton this afternoon?"

His voice had a deep bass to it. It echoed in the room. Hanging in the air and slowly dissipating after it seemed the time was right.

Where Stone's voice went the evil recoiled. As Maggie sobbed louder, it returned unable to resist.

"Your honor," fat man McGuire said. He wiped his upper lip on his sleeve again to continue.

Stone cut him off.

"Quiet," Stone's words were not loudly spoken. They were soft. His voice cut through the air like thunder though. Turning his attention and locking eyes again with McGuire then slowly down and over to Doug Marks the city prosecutor. Marks would not return the gaze.

Doug Marks was a drunkard. He had a large red nose and long greasy blond hair. The bailiff looked at Judge Stone. Stone nodded back while still glaring at the city prosecutor and his incompetence.

"The court recalls Missus Maggie Summers," the freeman bailiff spoke loudly and formally.

McGuire reseated in his defendant's chair. He had a very unpleasant smile fade across his face, underneath the dancing handkerchief.

With all eyes on her Maggie slowly stood up and walked to the front of the courtroom. She was a thin woman. Plain and weathered who looked like she had been attractive once. Life on the range had taken it from her.

The evil in the room danced around and out of her way. It seemed gleeful, looking forward to something. Maggie did not notice it.

After she sat down in the witness chair Judge Stone looked over at her, "Missus Summers," Stone asked in a soft voice that still carried to the back of the room and hit the back wall easy, "you got anything you want to clarify after we heard from Sheriff Burton this morning?"

Maggie composed herself. No small feat.

"Yes Judge," she said as she moved hair from her forehead with her left hand pushing it behind her ear. She looked as dignified as she could. Tried too.

"Your honor," McGuire said. He rose from his chair for a second time. The fat under his chin jiggled with the effort. McGuire had been a corporate lawyer for the railroad until six months ago. He had abruptly closed his practice and started working across several Colorado mining towns. Mostly working for wealthy railroad clients from Denver City. His appearance almost two hundred miles away in the mountain town Alamosa was a surprise.

Stone looked back at McGuire annoyed. Everywhere he looked the evil in the room hid, fearful of being caught in his gaze, "Take your seat council, you can relax we're following the book here. I ain't interested in no city lawyer trickery," it came out straight. "Let's all be given a chance to speak our truth."

"Missus Summers if you will," Stone said, unhappy with where he knew this was going. There was too much interest in this by the shadows for it to go well.

"Thank you Judge," Maggie said.

"I have been giving this all a lot of thought," she paused being introspective.

"Sheriff Burton says he saw me shoot my husband. In the back. When William was running after Mister McGuire here after he left our house," she was looking at McGuire.

"At first I did not have words," turning to Judge Stone, "I could not understand why he would say that. He claims he saw what actually happened," Maggie had calmed down a lot. She still seemed to be in shock, but she was managing herself well.

She looked out to the town people in the room, looking past McGuire, "Judge can I have some water?"

Judge Stone made a motion to the bailiff and after a few moments a porcelain pitcher and some small cups were brought in. Maggie took a cup and drank all of it.

While she drank the shadows danced.

"Then I started thinking, why?" She continued, "Why would he say that? Then I started thinking more. It does not make no sense. Mister McGuire shot William. He shot him when he turned his back on him after the argument about the land deed."

Maggie turned to Stone, "Why did he want that land so bad Judge?"

Stone looked back at her. It was a reasonable question and if Marks the prosecutor had any wits it is what they would all be talking about. Stone felt conflicted. He did not know what happened at the ranch. His job as a judge came with laws. His obligations with rules. He often had to balance both.

"Motive," Marks spoke softly as if from a daze. It broke the moment between Maggie and Stone.

"Motive," Maggie said back, it seemed she was trying the word out as it broke the spell.

"I ain't got no motive," Maggie said as though understanding something. "Mister McGuire does, he wants our land. I needed William to work the land and make our life. We were happy out there. Everyone here knows it."

There was a long pause and it seemed she was finished talking.

"Mister Marks," Stone said looking over at Doug Marks who still looked shell-shocked after his single utterance, "do you have anything to say before I turn the witness over to Mister McGuire?"

Marks as the city prosecutor had been out of his element since the trial started. Even though McGuire was acting as his own council, he was twice the lawyer Marks could ever be.

"No, your honor," Marks said in a defeated voice. The evil danced around him and consumed him until he was a shadow himself. If he had anything to offer it was gone.

Stone exhaled, reluctantly he spoke, "Your witness Mister McGuire."

Suddenly moving gracefully across the room for such a heavy man McGuire was standing between the empty jury box and the witness box in no time. He almost floated there, quickly, with the help of the shadows. Surrounded by darkness but as if in divine light. He gestured at Stone with a question. Waving his arm a bit to bring attention to the vacant jury section.

Stone noticed that damn handkerchief was back.

"This here is preliminary Mister McGuire. We'll bring them back in once I'm satisfied," Stone said with a thin humorless smile on his face.

"Of course, your honor," McGuire said with the same amount of false graciousness.

"Missus Summers," McGuire began quickly, he was nimble in thought and mannerisms once engaged in the court.

"Just yesterday you told us that the sheriff was not out at your place when all this happened," McGuire gestured to where the sheriff had been seated for most of the trial, "shooting your husband dead at your ranch a month gone.

"It was a terrible tale and we all felt the weight of it. You being alone and helpless after the shooting and all. Do you remember that?"

"Yes, I remember," Maggie said in a regal voice. Her head up and looking to the back of the courtroom not at McGuire.

"We all remember very well too," said McGuire. "You went on to say that me and William had a fight over the deed to your ranch. If my memory serves you were in default. Do you remember that also?"

Maggie turned to look at McGuire, twisting her head a bit and answering indignantly, "Yes, I remember that as well sir."

"We all remember," McGuire said again. You could feel him building up to something.

"And were you in default?"

Maggie said something softly.

"What did you say?" McGuire screamed. It was a quick change in mannerism and jolted everyone in the room. It was terrifying.

Maggie reacted as though she were physically hit. Maybe she was. She became outwardly scared.

"Were you present earlier today when Sheriff Burton testified?" McGuire yelled.

"Good lord sir you know I was," she snapped and yelled back sobbing again as her voice cracked, "you all know. I was the one yelling at him and calling him a liar while you went on with your pretty little story."

McGuire issued a singular chuckle that snapped into the room like an electric bolt.

Stone hit his gavel on the desk twice. He wanted to interrupt McGuire's building storm.

Maggie's low sobbing developed a rhythm. She tried to hold it back.

McGuire looked to Judge Stone to continue, and then up to Maggie a sort of mock apology by making a face he thought only she could see and shrugging his shoulders.

"So now we have a problem don't we," McGuire spoke in his normal voice. He was serious in his own way. He did not carry a room like Stone did but he currently spoke with righteousness and authority.

"We are forced to believe either myself, a good, honest, hardworking businessman. Here today based on your testimony. Alone. Friendless. Accused of murdering folks to collect their land deeds. On trial for my life. Or a woman who maybe only wanted to leave her life of hardship behind by getting rid of the person who was holding her here."

It did not gain sympathy with anyone but it somehow seemed to carry weight. "Preposterous," McGuire said slowly, allowing his Irish accent to shine through.

He continued without missing a beat, "Murdering your husband?" he yelled again looking up to the ceiling with his arms out. Saying the words as though they were impossible.

"May. I. Be. Struck. Down. If. True."

He paused dramatically still looking up to the ceiling of the room. His arms were outstretched. He was in the shape of a cross. The pause seemed genuine. It made it feel like he was telling the truth.

Then McGuire said quietly with full command of the moment, "As testified to by you," a definitive statement, accusatory. Full of spite. Spitting the words out.

"But who are we to believe?" he turned to the remaining townsfolk.

"A widowed rancher trying to save her own skin," he held up his left hand. "or the duly sworn town Sheriff who told a very different tale just a few short hours ago," McGuire's words cut hard and hit Maggie again like a slap as he held up his right hand.

"Why would I shoot a man that owed me money? Now I will never collect it!

"And if I am such a villain, why would I shoot William in the back in front of the town sheriff? And if it were only you and me, why would I not shoot you too? It would have finished my dastardly plot and actually released the land deed to me."

Stone believed him.

The comprehension came too late as he noticed that a few men, all roughly dressed the same, had started to meander into the courtroom and were spaced out around the back of the room. They all seemed to appear out of nowhere, wearing brown work pants and having something red on them, a shirt, vest, bandana, armband, gloves, something.

Before Maggie could respond to McGuire's question Stone spoke, "Bailiff, would you please clear the courtroom."

The room was silent. Nothing happened.

It slowly dawned on Stone that the bailiff was not in the room anymore.

"Maggie," Stone looked over at her as realization washed across his face.

He spoke in a low soft voice, "You better get on now."

Maggie looked at Stone and at the growing number of men in the room wearing red. She did not understand what was happening and was becoming more frightened.

"Maggie," Stone spoke again as he stood up and moved in her direction.

"If you don't get now," thunder in his voice as he started to run to her, "there ain't going to be no later."

The large courtroom erupted in chaos. There was gunfire and screaming. Walking over and sitting in his defendant's chair James McGuire smiled.

Darkness danced all around him.

Divine light shone and illuminated him.

BLACK ICE

A lamosa burned bright in the dark of night.

The rain and wind raged against the town like a hurricane.

Fire reflected in Stone's eyes.

Blood ran down from his right shoulder. A .22 caliber round had passed straight through. It left a bigger hole in the back than the front.

Standing up now that the fight was over, Stone stepped out from behind the makeshift barricade down the small alley. He had thought fast and found a strategic hold where he could return fire without anyone flanking him or the worry of crossfire.

He checked his rifle. The barrel was so hot steam would rise off the length of it every time a raindrop landed. Four hundred rounds had been fired by him within the past hour. Now only a few rounds were left in the fourteen-round magazine. The rifle was otherwise out of ammo.

Stone's sidearm was loaded and unused. It was still in its holster covered in a pink combination of Stone's own blood and rainwater. He knew the shoulder was going to be a problem. It always was. However right now it was just a dull numbing pain and his arm was still working fine against all logic.

Bleeding from three or four other grazes including one from a Colt .45 that had dug deep across his cheek and had maybe blown his ear off. He could still move and shoot as he needed.

He was powerful mad.

There was no one around to notice.

Between the scowl on his face and his bloody appearance he looked like wrath had come calling.

Alamosa looked like hell on earth. Dying amongst the wind and flames.

Around Stone were dozens of bodies. Townsfolk and McGuire's men had fallen in equal measure when it was all said and done. For the townsfolk Stone had been the only chance at salvation. For McGuire and his gang Stone was their only competent adversary. Both ended up systematically slaughtered by the other.

It had been a bloodbath with the gang riding into the town with a purpose. This had been no simple jailbreak.

As Stone now slowly walked from the alley onto the main street, he noticed many of the McGuire Gang lay dead around the area his barricade had been established. There were others here and there. A horse had dragged one a good way down the main street before the rider had fallen off, for example.

Maggie was dead. Stripped and hung from the front of

the courthouse about six feet off the ground. Black and blue in a bad way. She died with her hands still clawing at the noose ripping the skin of her throat. Her front was covered in her own dark red blood. What was left of her neck a little longer than it had been a few hours before.

The evil that had been interested in Alamosa no longer was.

It was gone, but something new was in its place.

The courthouse building was on fire. The rope that held Maggie's noose was on fire too.

It seemed almost everything was on fire in Alamosa.

In some places even the dirt.

Doug Marks the worthless town prosecutor was in a couple pieces down the Main Street. The gang had gone after him early. There were bodies and guts and blood everywhere and you could see everything good from the light of all the burning stuff. Even in the dark and through the rain.

The rain had washed away the earlier stink. It was working on washing away the repugnant sweet copper smell that had gathered in its place from all the blood and carnage.

The fires made everything orange. The rain made things shadowy. The wind kept the shadows dancing.

Some of the buildings burned on the outside like the church and hotel. In some you could see the fire inside like the dry goods store and the livery stable.

The rain got louder.

Stone was a silhouette in the middle of the street watching the town burn.

Wrath. Came. Calling.

The wind stilled, then picked up in bursts. Then Still.

He looked up into the dark clouds and let out a scream of rage and frustration. Either from the force of his yell or some other manifestation, the fire finally caused Maggie's rope to snap and she fell to the ground with a thud. Stone heard it but did not turn around to see it. There was no dignity in her death. Less for her now.

In a mocking response to his scream of frustration, the dark skies opened. It started to hail black ice as if to remind Stone that it can always get worse. He did not need the reminding. He welcomed the pain from the small round pellets as they struck about him.

Pain meant life.

Over the noise of the hail, Stone heard moaning.

He walked up the street and found McGuire in the mud. McGuire's leg at a wildly wrong angle and clearly broken. If not worse. There were several stab wounds bleeding through his filthy suit.

Stone smiled to himself a sad smile. The townsfolk were not gunmen and ultimately fell, but they were not sheep either and went down fighting. He put his foot on McGuire's mangled leg and pushed.

That brought the fat man awake screaming with little effort.

"McGuire," Stone spoke, his voice was otherworldly, too

much bass and anger in it. Even deeper now than before when in the courtroom, carrying easily through the noise of the night.

The rain and hail were coming down hard.

It took McGuire a few seconds to understand where he was. He looked up at Stone both pathetic and confused.

Stone took a breath and looked from McGuire to the burning town and dead townsfolk. Then looked back to McGuire who was starting to realize it was Stone's foot pressing into his broken leg that was a main cause of his distress.

The wind and hail whipped into a frenzy feeding off of Stone's anger. Accenting the pointless loss of life and the destruction of a town hard built.

This was not the petty small darkness from before. It was something grander. Larger. Hungrier.

The wind, it seemed, was angry that anyone was left alive. The rain mixed with the hail coming down so hard that most of the fires were going out.

The buildings were starting to buckle and fall.

Something evil was destroying Alamosa.

Nature was out of balance dancing about desperate for more madness.

Stone yelled at McGuire through the noise, "Why did you want the land?"

McGuire was in real pain and in a bad way, "Take your damn foot off my leg," he spat.

Stone pushed hard and McGuire screamed in pain again.

The wind picking up in glee as he pressed.

Stone removed his foot.

McGuire tried to right himself and succeeded to some degree, looking down at his mangled leg.

"Why did you want the land," Stone repeated. It did not come out so much as a question this time.

"I did not kill that man."

"That ain't what I asked you," Stone picked his foot back up and made a show to put it back on McGuire's leg.

McGuire panicked, "Gawd dammit Judge you know I did not kill that boy. I saw it in your eyes," McGuire was not pleading but it was close, "I am innocent. You know that."

Stone paused. Hung his head. Closed his eyes. He was centering himself and forcing patience.

"James, you sure as hell are not innocent. You are guilty as sin and twice as mean as any man I know. Maybe not guilty of murdering William but guilty of enough in this world. Who killed William Summers does not currently concern me."

Stone remained a silhouette. Two dimensional. "I am asking one more time. If you do not answer I ain't going to be nice like before. Why did you want the land."

"Times are changing, Judge. Things are being found out. The future is coming and it is meaner than you and me both together," McGuire looked up into the dark clouds.

"I am talking real power," he continued making eye contact with a wild look, "not this shadow mysticism crap.

I am talking about the power to destroy your enemies in
mass. From afar. The power to deal pain in ways you cannot understand. For generations at a time. To be a god,
not to serve one."

It was the truth and Stone knew it. But it did not tell him
anything.

The two men stared at each other for a few moments.

After a bit Stone gauged McGuire was done talking.

"That all you gonna give me James," he asked.

McGuire looked down at his leg. Tried to move it.
Winced, "Yes," knowing what it meant. He had the handkerchief back in his right hand waving it as if giving up.

The rain and hail were sideways.

Loud and fast.

A building collapsed making a huge crash.

Driven by the elements, switching his rifle to his left
hand in a fluid motion, Stone drew his six-shooter and
fired a single round into McGuire whose head partially
exploded immediately with the discharge.

As the report echoed out in a visible circle around him
the sound traveled slow making an expanding bubble in
the rain and wind. It met the roar of the weather and si-
lenced it.

Water and ice fell from the air where they were in an
instant.

As the report faded it left a new eerie wet silence.

The wind died in that instant too, the stark stillness hung

for a moment with an unspoken echo that was only interrupted by a soft voice from behind Stone.

"Sheriff Burton is heading to the Indian reservation," the voice said.

Stone dropped his head again.

He went through the same process of gathering himself.

Instead of turning around he forced himself to lift his head and look up the street in front of him.

Using the scene to rekindle the flames of his anger he checked the load of his rifle and remembered he was almost out of ammo. He replaced the single spent cartridge from his six shooter and reseated the chamber in the pistol.

"Would that be all of it then?" Stone said to the air behind him.

"Yes," the air behind him said, "here."

"Here?"

There was no reply. Stone started to take a step forward and then paused. Introspectively, "I'm sorry you were hanged Maggie," him meaning it.

"I know you are, Judge. I ain't as mad about it as I used to be," the air said.

"Seems to me it's still a current event," holstering his sidearm and still looking down the street at the ruined town.

The fires were mostly out.

Put out by the rain, wind, and hail.

The buildings dripped water. Here and there they continued to collapse and fall.

"For you, this, this is happening now," the air was soft and pleasant, easy to hear in the night, silent now except for the water that soaked everything which had a way of making its own noise. It filled in the spaces between the whispers, "it is hard sometimes for me to remember that."

Nothing happened for a while.

"Do you want to know about time, Judge? How it really works? Why it is hard for me to remember the now and differentiate it from the then?"

"No," said Stone.

Another long pause.

"For you," the air continued ignoring Stone's answer, "time is something you measure, something that tells you when to wake up and when to eat.

"Something that tells you when to die.

"But that's not it at all.

"Time is not a measure it is a motion.

"It is the motion of the universe. It is the most beautiful thing there is when you can finally step away from it. See it from a distance. Be free from its constant incessant ebb and flow.

"When I was freed from it, from time, I could move through the universe as easily as you can walk up this street."

"I don't care Maggie," Stone said, lowering his head again, "and between you and me walking up this street don't seem so easy right now."

"It will be," the air had gotten louder, "when I was alive, I thought that time was something that I wanted more of. When I was up on that rope I wanted more.

"I was a glutton for it trying to drink it like water. Breath it like air.

"As it left me, I resented its loss. I raged and hated its absence in every measure.

"The more it abandoned me the more I wanted it.

"I grew so angry that it was being denied to me.

"At the very end time was all I wanted. It was everything and the only thing that mattered.

"I would have given anything for just the tiniest bit more of it. In some ways I did.

"But now I know what it is, and I don't want it. Now I have all of it and I hate it completely.

"It is the most beautiful thing when you don't have it. The vilest when you do.

"I have all of it now and want nothing more than to be rid of it again.

"It is just a hollowed-out picture.

"A picture in a thousand empty frames on a thousand empty walls."

Stone was tired, "What do you want from me, Maggie."

"Justice," whispered the wind, fading away.

"I don't know what that is Maggie. Neither do you."

"You're a Judge, justice is what you do."

"No, being a Judge does not have nothing to do with justice. It has to do with the law. And even then, only partially."

The wind laughed, "Well, I know how all this ends. I know what justice is. I know you get justice for me and I am free of this curse called time forever."

"What is justice then Maggie?" Stone asked the wind.

"It is what you are bound to do for me Judge Stone."

"That going to end it all then. Justice?" Stone asked, hopeful.

"No," the voice was sad.

Stone paused as the moment ended and the whisper was gone.

It started to rain lightly, this time though a natural rain.

Cleansing.

"Justice never ends anything. It is always a new beginning," the wind whispered as it vanished into the night sky.

Stone did not care about the rain and was thinking about Maggie.

"Disappointing," he said as he finally started to walk up the street into what used to be the town of Alamosa, realizing that his shoulder hurt very badly. As he stepped over the remains of McGuire his foot landed on the dirty handkerchief smashing it into the wet mud.

Soon after he noticed that the air smelled pleasantly like a fresh summer evening.

DENVER CITY

Stone had never met Colonel Gus Maddox before today. He had never even heard of the man. But here Maddox was in the office of the Colorado Territory Marshal instead of Stone's friend Edward Hamilton.

Stone had worked his way through the mountains to Denver City. The weather agreeable and pleasant. The mountain air fresh and clean. It was a two-week trip. He made the Georgetown loop after twelve days then took the train the rest of the way. It gave him a couple days rest and he healed up surprisingly good on the trip back.

Upon returning he wanted to discuss matters with Hamilton before deciding what to do next. Intending to give a full report of the goings on and murderous rampage.

Small plots and villainous behaviors were not uncommon in the territory. But the magnitude of what happened in Alamosa exceeded even Stone's most wild post war experiences. McGuire was part of something. Had been. Something with enough resources and organizing ability to send a gang of heavily armed red shirts to commit mass murder.

McGuire had told him the truth there at the end.

He had said that times were changing. He also spoke about the shadows. Comparing the shadows as trivial to this new power.

It felt like McGuire was right. Things were changing.

Again.

Stone had made a bad deal a long time ago. One no one had ever made before. It changed everything.

He had never regretted it.

Not once.

Just because it was a bad deal did not mean it was not good for him.

Sometimes, but not always, he struggled to see the light through the dark.

The deal gave him time. Maggie had been right in her description of time too. At the very end, you want more of it. You would do anything for it. Almost.

In contrast to his introspection, Hamilton's office here in Denver City was comfortable and formal. Stone knew that his rugged sunburned and wounded appearance looked out of place in it.

Stone and Hamilton went way back. Back to before the American Civil War that ended over a decade ago.

The United States had fought a great war with itself from 1861 to 1865 between a coalition of northern states called the Union and seceded southern states called the Confederacy. Over a million soldiers and civilians were killed in the massive military conflicts and battles over the four years.

The Battle of Richmond was a battle late in the war. It was the last significant confederate victory. Ever.

At the battle Stone had led the final pointless Union charge at Cold Harbor, under the order of General Ulysses S. Grant. Grant was the commanding General of the Union army and went on to become President. He was currently running for reelection.

A few years after the war Grant had admitted to Stone, and others, that his only single regret was ordering the final charge at Cold Harbor.

The battle was a disaster for the Union. The men under Stone's command that were not killed in the needless show of devotion were captured. Shipped off to the hell hole Andersonville, a confederate prison.

Hamilton had been one of Stone's Captains. After the war he became one of Stone's good friends.

Both had prospered in the aftermath of the war. Stone taking a judicial appointment from President Grant. Hamilton working his way up to become the territory marshal for Colorado. It was a political post, voted on by the people in the territory in the last election and serving for six years.

Judge Stone leaned forward from the English style red leather chair. His right arm in a sling so his shoulder could heal. A fresh pink scare ran from his left cheek and split his ear, which was otherwise intact. The scar showed signs where stitches had recently been removed.

He looked old.

The fresh wounds and sling made him look weak.

He was neither but in truth Alamosa had been a hell of an ordeal.

On the wall were several wanted posters. Also, a map of the proposed new Colorado State, about a third of it, the western and southern section, given to the Ute as an Indian reservation.

The reservation was highlighted on the map.

Seated across from Stone in a similar leather chair sat Maddox.

Maddox's eyes were blue. His hair was blonde. His chin was chiseled. His voice was loud. His presence was commanding.

"What is it you want?", Maddox said in his loud voice sounding commanding.

"I'm looking for some help finding Sheriff Alvord Burton," Stone said. He spoke soft and calm but his deep bass voice made it seem louder than it was.

Maddox looked at Stone for a bit. Letting his blue eyes hold Stone as the two sized each other up. Leaving Stone's statement to echo and fade.

"Seems to me he fled Alamosa before the Indians attacked," Maddox said finally. Sounding commanding again. Seemingly putting the matter to rest.

"Colonel, I appreciate your perspective on things I really do. It does, however, remain unclear to me why you are here," Stone said looking at Maddox, "I came to speak to

Edward Hamilton. The actual territory marshal."

Maddox was unmoved. He grew even more bored in mannerism if that were possible. It seemed the question was expected and he casually leaned back in his chair and looked above Stone to the door.

"The Colonel," Hamilton appeared in the doorway behind Stone, "has been assigned as the head of the Colorado Territory Militia in anticipation of our Statehood. As such, Governor McCook has temporarily instilled state responsibility for some functions to the militia. Such as territory Indian affairs and overall peacekeeping."

Stone had to twist in his chair to see Hamilton. It was no easy task given his bad shoulder and the way the chair had been positioned. Irritation grew inside of him, "Indian affairs? What do the damn Indians have to do with what happened at Alamosa?" Stone asked. Not liking the change in focus and the way things were being orchestrated.

"Judge," Maddox leaned forward.

Stone had to twist back around to return his gaze at Maddox, who continued, "We have gotten word back from the platoon I sent up after the report. They assessed the situation and have informed me by telegraph that the town has been burned to the ground with everyone killed. They tell me it was clear that the Ute Indians had sent a war party to do the work."

Maddox was loud when he talked.

Stone was silent simply looking at Maddox who returned the gaze. Finally Stone spoke, "Colonel I have not given my report yet that is actually what I came here to do today," holding out hope that this was a real conversation.

The silence became uncomfortable and Hamilton spoke to fill it. Still standing behind Stone's chair he said, "That's the problem Judge. With no information other than from Burton's telegraph it has pretty much been concluded it was the Ute. There is a history of this on the western slope."

Hamilton walked around and sat in the leather chair next to Maddox across from Stone, "I spoke to Edward McCook, the Territory Governor myself."

Hamilton continued, "Politically, he needs it to be Indians. It gets the army here," a nod from Hamilton to Colonel Maddox, "and federal funding. The Governor thinks you have a personal vengeance and did not want to wait for information on your whereabouts," Hamilton looked down at his hands avoiding eye contact for the last part.

"That's ridiculous Ed and you know it," Stone said to Hamilton not knowing exactly what the angle was here and why Hamilton appeared to be Maddox's man. Stone knew he was not. He knew that whatever Hamilton was doing was in what Hamilton perceived to be Stone's best interest, so he continued, "The blasted Indian Agency is right down the street here in Denver. What you say makes no sense. They have a third of the territory. All Legal. They have a treaty."

Stone looked from Hamilton to Maddox. Thought some, "How can any of this have been decided? I just got back here today. There ain't no other firsthand witnesses with information could have made it back here faster."

The room started to fill in on Stone from the edges. He started to pick up the environment change. Not outwardly but under the air. Like shadows were coming but not exactly.

Maddox, seeing Stone lose focus, looked like a lion who had all the time in the world to take down his prey, "Judge, we ain't a state yet. Your federal," Maddox did not pause for an answer, "it seems to me you are out of your element. A man of your position, and age, should not need concern himself with the complexities of governing a territory."

Hamilton spoke up, having a slightly disapproving look cross his face that Stone could see but Maddox could not, "We received a telegraph from Burton right after, about two weeks ago."

Stone looked to the window reminding himself to remain civilized. Outside the sun went behind a cloud. Both the light and the mood darkened. He noticed that Maggie was standing in a corner of the room, watching, listening.

She had not been there a few minutes ago. That explained the disturbance he sensed.

"Well," Stone said looking straight at Maddox, "you have been given some bad information."

Maddox made a sound of disapproval.

Stone considered drawing his sidearm and shooting Maddox in the head. He knew he would eventually have to confront the man.

Doing it now would be easy and quick.

The look crossed Stone's eyes and Maddox noticed it.

But Stone had no justification. He needed justification. From this world or the next. Those were the rules.

The moment passed.

Instead, he hoped to provide an opportunity for Maddox to set himself on an honest path, "Seems to me there are some implications if the governor ain't taking the time to listen to a federal judge," Stone said, "and if said governor ain't interested in the federal Judges whereabouts after a massacre like this."

Stone pulled his gaze from Maddox and looked back at the ghost, purposely very neutral in tone, "but it's also interesting how quick the military was able to wrap the whole affair in a bow with a predetermined decision," Stone spoke soft, but it came out hard, and you listened when he spoke this way.

Maddox leaned back in his chair, seemingly interested in Stone for the first time. When Maddox spoke again his voice was different, still commanding but speaking to Stone more as a peer.

"As a Judge, you concern yourself with applying justice after the fact," Maddox said ready to continue.

"Well Colonel, begging your pardon, as a Judge I concern myself mostly with what's legal and what's not so legal," Stone interrupted.

Maddox stopped and thought, "I accept that. However, are you suggesting that the law and what's required for justice are not the same thing?"

Stone smiled thinly, "Are we changing the conversation to philosophy? I was more interested in you answering my question concerning your unit's quick intelligence work."

"Let me rephrase," Maddox said as though at a dinner party, "as a Judge, you listen to the stories of other people and then apply judgement after the fact. In hindsight. That is the point I was going to make. You are one step removed from the consequences of people's actions."

Maddox's voice softened even more, then hardened at the end of his statement, "I was going to suggest that you attempted to apply justice after the fact. Believing it to be the same as the law. As I do. But now I wonder what you believe. What kind of good for nothing judge you might actually be."

Hamilton gave Stone a pleading look, knowing his nature.

Stone trusted Hamilton and decided to indulge him and let the insult pass. For several reasons and to learn something about Maddox as a man. He looked over at Maggie standing in the corner of the room and looked at her face as he spoke next. She looked older than he remembered.

"I believe being a federal Judge has many complexities Colonel. It is interesting you bring up justice. That seems to be a topic of some interest lately.

"I would be happy to discuss this subject with you at some future point in time.

"In today's conversation I'll keep it simple and say that of the many complexities involved in being a federal Judge, being disconnected from the consequences of people would not be one of them," Stone smiled a thin smile.

Maggie looked at him from the shadows.

She suddenly looked younger than she had been at the end of her life. Not young like a girl just less weathered. Her hair was combed well, and her blue dress looked pressed and washed.

Maddox was dismissive, "Of course you believe that I have no doubt. That is the difference between a person who relies on society for safety like you and a military man like myself. I live in a world of action and consequence governed by a pursuit of justice. You live in a world where your basic needs are provided for. Where strong men like me protect you from your own folly."

Stone looked over to Hamilton quizzically.

Hamilton returned an uncomfortable shoulder shrug.

Stone had served in the Union army for a decade. Maddox should know this. Most everyone knew it. It must mean Maddox did not come from federal military service. Or, that he had not fought in the civil war. At least not on the side of the Union. It also probably meant he gave Stone no regard whatsoever.

Stone was genuinely curious. An old feeling he had not experienced in a while, "Colonel, if I may, you believe the difference between you and me is that you are a military man of action and consequence. That making this point will somehow help you answer my original question about the timing of your decision to blame the Ute Indians for Alamosa?"

Maddox spoke loud, like instructing a child, "I want to help you, Stone. Help you understand how the world works. Things ain't like you remember. Times have changed. The old ways are over. Your day has passed.

"My day is here.

"Out with the old, in with the new.

"When I tell you something, your job is to do it.

"Your job is to believe it. Believe it because you heard it from me. Because I spoke it, therefore it is your truth.

"You say law and justice are not the same thing.

"I am telling you that they are.

"There, problem solved. I have enlightened you.

"If you would like to borrow one of Hamilton's fancy pens you can write that down and put it in your pocket."

Maddox snorted then leaned forward, showing energy for the first time. Speaking loud and commanding, "Look at you, you are an old, beaten man. Look at me. I am in my prime. Strong. Quick. Better.

"As such, if I tell you the sky is blue, the sky is blue.

"If I tell you it ain't, it ain't.

"If I tell you law and justice are the same, they are the same. Only if I tell you they ain't, they ain't.

"If I tell you the Ute attacked Alamosa.

"The. Ute. Attacked. Alamosa.

"If I tell you that old men should spend their time worrying about old men's problems, your job is to do that,"

DAVID EDWARD

Maddox said dismissively. He was spent. He seemed to believe he had just taken the time to deliver wisdom and sat back in his chair.

There was silence for a good while.

Maddox was in the afterglow of his speech and was willing to wait however long it took for Stone to respond.

Stone considered shooting Maddox a second time. Even though he did not like the man, nothing in the rules had changed in the last ten minutes so he could not. Or at least did not.

Hamilton looked unsure, poised to spring if necessary although to what end Stone could not discern.

Seeing no other option Stone finally said something, "Colonel," in an even tone looking at Maddox, "I am not certain at all that you and I are going to get along here."

The response broke the spell.

Maddox stood up and when he spoke again it was back in his original loud voice, "Sir that will be your loss," he walked across the room and to the door, "you have been given a choice Stone. You can do as I tell you. You can do something else. You seem of no consequence to me.

"Your choices are simple, and you are lucky I found you interesting enough to offer you a choice at all."

With that Maddox was gone. The room was silent again for a long while.

Finally, Hamilton spoke up to fill the silence.

"Things are political now Judge. It is the new way," Hamilton said.

"What has Governor McCook gotten himself into?" Stone asked disapprovingly.

"I wish I knew," Hamilton said as he stood up and made a gesture to the door.

Stone stood up and looked over to where Maggie had been, but she was gone now.

"Six hundred fifty," he said, finally looking back at Hamilton. Resolute but introspective. The world had changed a lot in the last twenty minutes. In that Maddox seemed to have been correct.

"What? Oh, of course I figured you may need a trip to the old bank," Hamilton said, seeming to understand the reference.

"Outside of the obvious here, are you still with me?" Stone asked.

"Of course," Hamilton said, making eye contact, "but I'm out on this one there is a lot of weird politics and maneuvering going on that I am still working to figure out. I ain't gonna be much help for the next little bit."

Before Stone left, they shook hands, Stone using a back handed left grip since his right arm was still in the sling.

COLD COFFEE

I t was a lot hotter outside than it had been an hour ago.

The downtown street was wide and busy.

People, horses, and drawn carts were going both ways. Up and down the thoroughfare in a bustle. There was a lot of racket and hammering on the edges. Denver City was growing fast.

Coming from Hamilton's office, Stone walked across the wide dry dirt street. He crossed from the government buildings into a cafe on the other side. Restaurants and eateries were showing up near office districts all over Denver City.

Stone entered and sat down at a table near the back. It was too small for him but he had a good view of the front door and was near an exit in the rear. He asked for a coffee from an unattractive French woman.

The inside of the cafe was temperate and crowded. The floor black and white squares. Green plants hung in a few places. The walls were a deep forest green color. It was nice. A large glass window in the front let light in. You could see the bustle outside easy.

Stone thought a bit about Maddox. The man seemed driven and had an agenda that needed observing. Unlike Maddox's assessment, Stone was neither helpless nor dismissible. Not to the extent Maddox seemed to believe anyway.

Stone knew also that he could just walk away. His next circuit schedule was for the loop ending at Steamboat Springs in a month and there was a lot of preparation to be ready. If he really were linked with a spirit again, he knew that he would need to see Maggie's journey to the end or she would remain earthbound and remain tied to him, which he did not want for her or for himself.

When the coffee came it came hot with two sugar cubes on the side in a white porcelain cup on a saucer. Sugar cubes were the latest in a line of new inventions. Before he could drink any of his coffee, a man wearing a well-tailored business suit in a modern style approached and sat down next to him at the table.

"Who drinks hot coffee at four in the afternoon on a scorching day like this?" the man asked.

"What kind of man wears nine layers of shirts at four in the afternoon on a hot day like this?" Stone responded without looking up. It was friendly banter and a nice break from his inner thoughts.

The businessman looked down at his clothes and dusted them off, happily presenting his suit, "It's all the rage."

Stone gestured to his coffee then swept his left arm to show the other people in the cafe drinking coffee, "It's all the rage," nodding to them and looking back at his cup, ready to pick it up and drink some. He did not get the chance.

"How'd it go?" A new visitor asked and sat down at the third and final chair around the little table.

The new visitor could not look more different from the businessman. He wore cowboy clothes and carried two big old colt sidearms. He still had his spurs on his boots. When he sat down, he slapped the businessman in the back as a friendly greeting and more dust came off the business suit.

"Edward is still one of us, but he's working in a bigger tent now and can't see past his nose so he's got to spend some time working stuff out," Stone said, and considered reaching for his coffee cup a third time but Jack Abbott, the cowboy, got agitated and began waving his arms, initially to clear the dust but then to make his point. It was a continuous motion with a smooth transition. Any attempt to pick up the coffee cup would be an exercise in one armed dexterity.

"If you're telling me that after all we've been through, Ed doesn't believe you," Abbott was getting visibly upset.

"It ain't that Jack so calm down," Stone said, "things are changing. It's all politics now."

The businessman, Dutch Levine, interjected "No offence Judge, but how is what happened at Alamosa political?"

Stone thought for a few moments, "Well," Stone spoke in his soft voice, the real serious one, the one you listened to, "as it was just explained to me, if you got no witnesses, it can be anything you want, so political. And the same way, if you got only one witness who will say whatever you want them to say, it can still be anything you want. So even more political."

"Uh huh," both Abbott and Levine agreed at the same time.

Abbott pondered the situation, "Wait a second. I thought you just said Hamilton believes you. Who is get 'n disbelieved then?" Abbott was smart, but not book learned.

"Of course he believes me. What is not to believe. We all go way back. You know that. You both go back just as far as he does. We all got the same secrets," Stone said while looking at his coffee cup. "Politics ain't about what's true. It is about getting folks to believe what you tell them so you can get what you want from them," Stone leaned in and continued, "But the real pickle is this fella named Maddox. He is a Colonel in some type of federal state hybrid militia. As far as I can tell. He wrapped the whole event up into a bow and got Governor McCook to sign off that it was the Ute Indians. It is done. I did not get back in time."

"Burton?" both Abbott and Levine at the same time.

"Burton, he sent a telegraph. Or at least they claim he did there ain't no real way to know who those things come from," Stone reached for his coffee and took a sip. It was cold by now and tasted bad. He made a face.

"Coffee here ain't no good huh?" said Levine, seeing Stone stop drinking, "Surprised given all the fuss. I had been meaning to check it out."

"Sugar's good," Abbott said, reaching over and taking the small sugar cubes from Stones coffee saucer and popping them both into his mouth at once.

"The telegraph gave Maddox everything he needed," Stone put the coffee cup down and pushed the saucer away.

"Maddox or McCook what they needed?" Levine asked.

"It's a good question Dutch. I cannot get my head around what the angle is. I am missing something obvious. Alamosa has put blinders on me," Stone concluded.

"So, what did happen up there?" Abbott asked when the opening came.

Stone was introspective for a bit. Abbott and Levine could see he was working up an answer so they stayed quite waiting. Finally Stone spoke, "Well, as far as I can tell the Irish had some land scheme. I do not know how high up it went and if Governor McCook is involved. The fat lawyer McGuire had a lot of Irish workers union help; I say he had help because I killed about thirty of them. It was the red shirts.

"They came in hard with two diversions and I honestly could not tell you if their goal was to free McGuire or kill everyone involved. It was a bloodbath and I was lucky to have survived it. The townsfolk fought hard and were near the match for them. I was the difference, but not by much. In the end, did not work out well for anyone.

"For Maddox, I can tell you he is full of himself in a way that suggests to me he has backing from some powerful political allies. He seems hell bent sure that he can do no wrong.

"It could be Governor McCook or someone else. Maddox ain't worried about anything federal getting in his way,"

Stone finished.

"You're federal," Levine said.

"Yep, and he sure ain't worried about me," said Stone with a thin humorless smile, "if McCook ain't involved then Maddox is a fool or he is taking orders and doesn't care. I guess either way that makes him a fool."

"This all seems pretty convoluted, shouldn't we just steer clear?", Abbott asked again.

"It's another good question," Stone thought for a few more moments, "I think I care for two reasons. First one is personal. Second one is that I think Maddox is part of something that is going to hurt a lot of innocent people."

"Sure," Levine said, "but I don't remember you being anointed the patron saint of Colorado any time recently."

"It's funny you would put it like that Dutch," Stone said, "because I am starting to feel like I might just be."

"What would we do? I do not see how we can accomplish anything meaningful. Even if we are onto something, Maddox has an army and McCook has the territory law," Abbott asked.

Levine spoke up, "I have heard rumors that the Irish are working on some type of deal where they are going to try and move something secret and valuable. Something on Indian land. I don't know what it is or even where they are trying to move it from, or to, but I have heard it is dangerous."

"Dangerous how," asked Stone.

"It's not really clear, but there is talk of people getting

powerful sick, getting boils, and dying just a few days after trying to take whatever it is. I am hearing some people complain that we gave the Indians the good land for their reservation. Talk of taking it back," Levine said.

"I have not heard anything about this," Abbott said.

"I hear through some back channels, you know what I am talking about," Levine said to Abbott.

"Oh, the secret order of the grapefruit," Abbott said softly poking fun at his friend.

"Knights of Gryphon Jack, and it ain't a secret group," Levin said, sounding irritated.

"Then why can't I join?" Abbott asked, some seriousness and possibly some history.

"You can join but you got to wear a suit and you have to pay the dues Jack."

It seemed an old argument may return so Stone said, "Okay fellas I don't have the energy to go through this again so let's drop it."

They sat in comfortable but anticipatory silence for a few minutes.

Stone stood, threw two pennies on the table, and headed for the door. The other two followed right behind him.

Outside the cafe the three men started to walk south down Broadway.

There were stores and businesses but much of the bustle of earlier in the day had died away.

The street was dirt dry due to the lack of summer rainstorms so far this year on the eastern side of the continental divide.

The late afternoon sun was still up above the mountains in the west and casting long shadows. The sky was a clear blue. The air was fresh. It was a nice afternoon.

"So, if I understood everything, we ain't just walking away from this. Right?" Abbott asked as they walked.

"I'm thinking I'm going to bring Burton back here to Denver as a live witness," Stone said as a matter of fact, "telegraphs don't make for good conversation."

"Going to need some gun hands," Levine said.

Abbott looked happy, "You can count me in," he said with a note of excitement.

Stone knew Abbott had a thriving horse farm and a family, "Wife and kids gonna be okay with that Jack?"

Abbott smiled, "Oh I think so. The boys are full grown. They pretty much run the ranch and business. I been home for a long while now. I think Martha might not mind me taking a short trip out for a couple weeks."

As Levine started to speak, Stone cut him off. He knew Levine would go if asked. Stone also knew Levine was not a trail man anymore. Stone did not want to put Levine on the spot. Unlike Abbott, Levine would better serve things staying here in Denver City.

"Dutch, I need you to go to our favorite old bank and make a withdrawal. We're gonna need some feed money," Stone said, showing no sign he noticed the expression of relief on Levine's face.

"Of course, Judge. How much?" Levine said, starting to

run numbers in his head.

"I'm thinking Jack and I make two solid lead operators. We will need two more who are really good. Maybe one of those that can track which will be extra," Stone said.

"OK, I'll bring back five hundred," Levine said, writing on a slip of paper 'Five hundred withdraw, gun hands, Dutch Levine', "Do we need to let Edward know?"

Stone looked up to the mountains far off in the distance.

The brim of his hat cut a line of shade that kept his grey eyes just out of the afternoon sunlight.

Even though it was a hot sunny afternoon he thought maybe he could see some darker clouds just behind the highest mountain peak racing the dusk, "I already told him we'd be taking for gun hands. He was not happy about it. But he understood."

A long pause as they continued to walk down the street.

"Jack, you still heeled with those ancient Colt Dragoons?" Stone finally asked, he could see Abbott was as the guns were large and obvious.

"Yep," said Abbott, getting excited because he knew where this was going.

"Dutch, do another slip there for $150 of miscellaneous," Stone said.

"Hamilton already knows?" Abbott said.

"Yep. Six hundred fifty. I already told him," Stone stopped walking and stood looking down the street.

"Jack," he said, "I think you and I need to go shop 'n."

WOLF & CO.

T he sign said, 'G. Wolf & Co.'

The building was big and brand new. It had large windows where you could see some displays on the inside.

Stone and Abbott walked in. There was a long counter on the right-hand side with an older bald man standing behind it. He looked up when they walked in, "What can I help you fine gentlemen with? My name is Mr. Wolf."

"We're looking for some new cartridge revolvers," Abbott said, excited. He put his poker face on when Stone looked at him sideways.

"Excellent. We have several to choose from. I typically recommend the Colt Peacemaker. The Army adopted it two years ago to good results," Wolf reached behind his counter and placed a new boxed Colt on the counter.

He then reached under again and produced a Remington box, "However, I just received some brand-new Remington Improved Army single action. It seems to be a superior product to me, but the prices are about the same."

"What's about?" asked Stone.

"The Colts are seventeen each, the Remington's twenty. They both fire .45's and hold six shots," noted Wolf.

"Can we try 'm?" Abbott asked.

About thirty minutes later both Stone and Abbott returned from the back alley. A small area had been set up to test firearms.

"We'll take the Remington's," Abbott said excitedly to Wolf.

"Good choice sirs. So that will be two Remington Improved Army revolvers."

"Four," said Stone, "and two of those five-dollar seven shooter pocket pistols."

"Good choice sirs," That phrase seemed to be Wolf's standard line, "will there be anything else?"

Stone handed him a list written in pencil on one of Levine's slips of paper, "Here is the rest of our list. Jack will stay here and coordinate with you. I have to get to the telegraph office before it closes. Do you know Dutch Levine?"

"Of course, sir, everyone knows Mr. Levine here in Denver City," said Wolf.

"Great. He will be here tomorrow afternoon to settle up with you," Stone said as he left the store.

Jack Abbott was beaming with excitement as he looked at the list together with the bald proprietor.

It was dark outside and less hot, approaching warm.

There was heat lightning off in the distance. Probably the clouds Stone had seen earlier. No thunder and no rain though.

The moon shone bright and it was easy to see.

Stone entered a building with a sign in the front that said 'Medical, T. Elwood. M.D.'.

Inside Tyler Elwood MD's medical office it was clean and smelled of disinfectant. The office was well lit from two very bright oil lamps.

After a bit Elwood had Stone sit on a table, take his arm out of the sling, and take his shirt off. The shirt part took a few minutes.

Elwood stood behind Stone examining the .22 exit wound in his shoulder.

"It's healed nicely and there is no infection. There is a lot of scarring on this shoulder from past wounds. That probably helped. It looks like the collar, shoulder, and your upper arm bone are all still out of joint though," the doctor said.

"Feels that way," Stone said.

"So, I'm going to have to put them all back into their joints."

"Seems appropriate." Stone said.

"It's going to hurt."

"What don't Doc," Stone said.

Elwood carefully lifted Stone's arm and positioned it just off to the side. Then suddenly he pulled it up while pushing against Stone's back. It sounded like the fourth of July with cracking for a second then immediately felt better.

Afterwards Stone walked up Broad Street. He headed to the Grand Union Hotel where he kept a room. The hotel was exceptionally large and very new. Eastern amenities were starting to make their way west. It had indoor plumbing and running water. You never needed to leave your floor if you did not want to.

It was seven floors high. A skyscraper.

There were no messages for him at the front desk so he went to his room. When he entered Maggie was there sitting in a straight back chair next to a small desk.

Well, sitting is not the right term but it is close enough.

"Do you want me to tell you about Maddox?" she asked Stone.

He could hear her voice in his head and see her in the chair. But it was not like talking to a regular person. The room was cold even though the night was still warm.

"Maggie, I do not need you always wanting to tell me about things. Things I do not care about. I think I understand Maddox well enough," Stone replied. Over the past week he had grown more accustomed to having conversations with Maggie.

Having a spirit attached to him was not necessarily something that was new. Since his escape from Andersonville he had dealt with half a dozen such attachments. Although, this was the first one that was female.

Maggie continued dismissing Stone's reply, "He sees you as a threat," she stated.

"He sees a lot of things as threats I would imagine," Stone said, taking off his boots and sitting at the foot of the large well-made bed.

"He did not see you that way at first but then something changed."

"Maggie, I appreciate the help and you looking out for me. I understand this all just fine. I have dealt with men like Maddox all my life. I just ain't in much of a mood currently to be talking to a ghost," Stone said, tired, rotating his right shoulder to try and get some of the stiffness out. It made soft popping noises when he moved it.

"Maddox sees himself as the next Governor. Once we become a state," Maggie said, continuing to ignore Stone's request to end the conversation.

Stone sighed. He summoned the energy to get through the conversation, knowing that she wouldn't stop until whatever it was she had to say was said, "So Maddox sees me as a threat to him becoming Governor. He did not feel that way until halfway through our conversation with him, right?"

"No. He believes that he is pursuing a destiny. He believes he is on some type of divine mission. I mean that literally. He believes that God has sent him on a mission," Maggie had become very defined in the chair, looking almost alive, "and he sees you as a threat to it."

"God don't send folks on missions Maggie. I got that info firsthand. I, alternatively, do assign missions. Currently I am on a mission to avenge a widowed ghost," Stone said wearily.

"You know that's not how this works," Maggie was now over focused and was more of a white light than a person, "you have to bring me justice not avengement. I have nothing to do with this whole mess beyond that."

"Sounds downright wholesome," Stone said nearing sleep.

"I believe Maddox is going to try and kill you," the light over the chair said.

"Of course. Maggie, that ain't news. I am probably going to end up trying to kill him too. So everything is in balance."

"Judge you don't understand. Things ain't in balance right now. Just me being here, bound by time again, has put things out of balance. But I do not matter all that much, neither of us does. The balance of the universe is off a great deal.

"When I finally died after all that time on the rope I went through a change. I do not know how to explain it. As a transition from this place to the other place, I guess. I suddenly found myself floating and moving towards a giant wheel in something like the sky at nighttime only much bigger. I could see other souls moving to the wheel too.

"We were all floating in from one way or another. Off in the distance I could see souls heading away leaving the wheel.

"Even though they were heading in a different direction from me, I knew that they were really heading back the way they had come. As far as I could tell there were more souls leaving the wheel than entering it.

"It was a stunning and beautiful sight.

"It took a real long time to get to the wheel. I do not know how long but if I had to guess I would say maybe all the time I was on the rope. Which seemed like forever to me. It took forever to get there.

"As I traveled, I realized that I was not traveling. I was not moving a distance. I was traveling through time. I realized that time and place were the same thing.

"If I went faster, then time went faster. The wheel spun faster, and I changed places faster moving closer. If I moved slower time went slower, and the wheel spun slower. I even tried going backwards. I tried it a few times and sure enough the wheel spun backwards. Time went backwards as my location moved away from the wheel.

"But I could only move away for a short period. I could choose to move away but if I lost focus, I moved closer.

"Then I understood. The souls I saw were not moving through space they were moving through time. Just like me. Some were still alive. Some had passed like me and could see what was going on. How we were moving to the wheel.

"I realized I had been moving to the wheel my whole life. Even before. I just did not know it. I could not see it. But now I could.

"The closer I got the more afraid I got. I could see more details. It was a giant machine. This was all a process. Life was just the movement to the wheel. Death was just the movement to the wheel. It was all the same.

"I could see that some souls entered the wheel and were rejected. They started their trip back in the same instant they arrived

"Some entered and vanished. I thought I heard screams in my head. Quick, but millions of them all at once. All the time. It was awful. I started to think I would disappear and for a while I screamed too. On my journey. I think at times I may have screamed for decades.

"As I got even closer I could see some souls entering and golden workers pulled them apart. Splitting them into two or three parts. Then sending them out to return. I could see the souls were in pain when they were split up. Those souls screamed for longer than the ones that disappeared.

"It was terrifying.

"There were also different parts of the wheel. Different parts moving in different ways and doing different things. I do not know how to put it into words. It was a very complicated machine but I could see all of it even though it was so large.

"For a long time before I got too close, I thought I was going to hell. I could not explain it any other way. What I saw happening to most of the souls was hellish.

"Then when I got there everything was white and pretty. But much of what was happening was horrific. I suddenly realized heaven and hell were the same place. No, that is not right this was not heaven or hell. Whatever this place was it was before that kind of judgement about good or evil. It served both heaven and hell the same way is what I meant.

"It served some other purpose too. It was some other measurement."

Stone leaned up on his good elbow and listened.

He made it a point not to care or listen to spirits because they only deceived. But he had to admit Maggie was being engaging here and was trying to tell it like it was.

Maggie continued not noticing Stone just having to get her story out.

"As I entered the wheel and passed from the outside to the inside, in that single transition, that single instant I was free. I could go anywhere. Move anywhere through time. And I did.

"I went everywhere and saw so many amazing things. People in other places. Different people in the same place. Since time did not matter to me, I could move any distance and be anywhere whenever I wanted.

"Then after a lot of trips the universe ended. It all just stopped.

"I was suddenly back in the wheel where I entered, only on the inside not the outside. It had only been a tiny measure of distance to transition from the outside to the inside. The smallest amount possible. So small it was almost between movements.

"But it was an eternity for me moving from the outside to the inside. I lived a thousand lives and saw a thousand possibilities.

"The golden works started to come for me and I started to scream again. I was so afraid. But before they could reach me I saw a light flash.

"Then suddenly I felt the pull of time and I started to get so heavy I could not stand it.

"Then I was behind you up in Alamosa again.

"I had been there hundreds of times after I died when I was in the between. But when I saw you this time it was the first time. The first time I had been there again since I died. It is hard to explain using words you can understand.

"As I sit here now bound to this place and unable to move. All I can do is watch time move things around me.

"I feel trapped.

"I am trapped.

"Even though I have seen all these things a hundred thousand times. More. This is the first time so those are just shadows of things that didn't happen anymore.

"It's hard for me to remember things and to remember what I have told you already and what I haven't yet. When we have talked this time versus the other times which were the same but were not now.

"I don't ever remember telling you all this. I actually do not think I am supposed to. But, if I am telling you now, I must have told you before. It must be ok because I am telling you again."

Stone picked up on an actual point to her ramblings and asked about it, "How are things out of balance?"

Maggie's light darkened when he asked, then returned to brightness. But not as bright as before, "It has got something to do with Alamosa. On the other side, with the wheel, they are not supposed to be splitting the souls up.

"The golden workers are supposed to be welcoming them. Helping them. Not hurting them.

"There is a repercussion to it all. It is breaking something, but I don't know what."

Stone asked, "How can a little mining town like Alamosa put the entire universe out of balance?"

The light above the chair was waning, "It cannot of course. It does not mean anything. But something happened there that day that did. I don't know what."

"Maggie," Stone asked, "is anything you just told be even remotely true?"

"You know how this works," she said nearly spent, "the words don't work right. But I tried to tell it straight."

"So, tell me. Something where the words work. That is true. Anything. For example, why is it always so cold when you show up?" Stone asked.

"Because the wheel is cold," Maggie said after she was gone.

BAD FOOD

It was a long day ride up from Denver City through the mountains to Nevadaville. Strange dreams from the night before still haunted Stone.

The trail up the mountain range ran along Clear Creek. The watercourse was a creek in the summer and a river in the spring. As rain had been scarce lately it was very much a creek right now. You could see the fingerprints of how it powerfully cut the mountains in the spring months as you rode up the canyons and gorges.

The mining companies had started working on building a train to bring gold ore from Blackhawk. The city of Blackhawk was a refinery town that employed thousands of workers.

This made the start of the trip slow and through a lot of commotion.

Judge Stone and Jack Abbott each rode on big Morgan Colts that belonged to Abbott. The Morgan horse is a sturdy all-purpose animal, at home galloping on open ground or making its way up rocky mountain trails full of packs. Abbott had collected several dozens of them after the war. They had been used as cavalry mounts by both the Union and the Confederacy. Near Washington D.C where Abbott had ended the war there were more horses than riders at the very end. Over the past decade Abbott had turned those fifty some horses into a solid business after moving to the Colorado territory. A good solid living. Not flashy but he had everything he wanted. Good wife, good boys, good land.

Today, each horse carried full travel packs and sleeping mats as well as their rider.

Abbott, as ever, was dressed in cowboy clothes. These clothes were in better condition than his normal fair having just been purchased yesterday. He wore a white work shirt, brown vest, blue jeans, and a brown three-quarter duster. He still wore his old Biggs cowboy hat. A good hat was hard to come by.

Stone on the other hand had dressed his mood. He had latitude as this was not an official federal trip. He wore a black shirt, black vest, black paints, a full-length black leather duster, and his black hat was a new style called a Dakota. A Dakota hat was a cross between a cowboy hat and a bowler. Stone looked intimidating. If he looked the part of a Judge before he now looked the part of a gun-fighter.

"Judge, you and I been ride 'n together for a long time," Jack Abbott said after an hour or so of silence, "I have seen you put your life on the line to right a single wrong, but also seen you kill men who probably did not do much wrong in the grand scheme of things other than break the law."

Stone turned his head sideways to look at Abbott quizzically.

Abbott saw the look and clarified, "For example when you took down the Bosher gang a couple years ago back in Kansas. You shot a lot of 'm. You could have brought them in for justice legal like. They were wanted alive even though they were charged with murder after all."

Stone looked up at the trail ahead, "You asking me which kind of trip we are on now?"

"I wouldn't mind know 'n," Abbot said.

"You and I ever talk about that before?" Stone asked, his quizzical look fading. His deep bass voice soothing.

"Sure," Abbott said, "a couple times."

"But it is still hard to tell?" Stone asked.

"Judge, I ain't privy to whatever it is that drives you. To me all these situations seem the same. I ain't opposed to kill 'n you know that. But l ain't going out looking for it either," Abbott offered.

"Jack, whenever I can I apply man's laws. Whenever I cannot I apply divine chastisement. But it ain't often up to me. If they sinned against man, we deal with it. If they sin against God, well, they bring about their own judgement."

"It's hard to reckon how you choose which is which Judge."

"I ain't the one who does the choosing Jack. Things get sorted out the way they come in. How many times you figure I done something like that which you might consider hard to figure?"

Abbott thought for a few minutes, "Counting Alamosa I would say six or seven times."

"Six or seven times, Counting Alamosa," Stone said back to Abbott.

"Yep."

"Like Alamosa," Stone said.

"Yep," said Abbott, "I ain't counting during the war none. Them was different times and none of it good."

They rode on for a bit then Abbott continued, "You are a scary cowboy. I've known you for most of my adult life and you strive to be balanced and helpful, going out of your way to avoid kill 'n except when you don't. You have a reputation as one of the most lenient judges on the circuit. Then out of nowhere you will shoot thirty gang members killing them all. And spend two months hunting down any survivors."

"I didn't shoot thirty of them Jack. Those mining towns are tough. You know that. They took each other out mostly. I did help some for sure, and I was the odds maker no doubt. The rest, well, it is actually complicated," Stone said back to Abbott.

"Well, I did not figure it was simple," Abbott said back quickly.

"Sometimes my job is to rule in a court of law with impartiality, as you note," Stone was looking off in the distance again as they rode, "sometimes I let things go one way. Then after a while, sometimes, I got to bring things back the other way."

The two riders could start to smell Blackhawk long before they could see it. It was an industrial town full of smelting and ore refining. Smoke and chimneys filled the valley.

Every tree in sight had been cut down.

Everything was covered in soot.

It smelled terrible.

"But based on what Judge? I don't understand how you make these decisions," Abbott said, pulling his bandana up over his mouth and nose to help with the smell.

"It's complicated," Stone said again.

"How so," Abbott said, not wanting to push too hard but also wanting to know what drove his friend.

"You ever see that French Lady with the blindfold? The one holding the scale?"

"Sure Judge, it's supposed to mean that the law is equal based upon the evidence. That right is right and wrong is wrong no matter who done it and who they did it to. And that judgment is supposed to be based upon the action not the person"

"Well, did you ever think about why she is holding a scale?"

"What do you mean," Abbott felt Stone was willing to tell him something here, so he was paying close attention.

"What does a scale do?"

"It tells you if something on one side weighs more than

something on the other side."

"And what's the scale the lady is holding saying?"

"It's even, so everything on the one side weighs the same as everything on the other side."

"Right," Stone said, seriously, "so while the lady and the scale are a metaphor, what it is trying to show is that the law is meant to bring balance to both sides, and the blind fold is telling you that to bring balance, you got to treat everything equal in the eyes of the law."

"So, justice is blind?" Abbott said, trying to understand the point.

"Gawd dang-it Jack we ain't talking about justice here. We are talking about the law. Why, confound it, is everyone obsessing over justice all of a sudden. Man does not know justice. Much less how to know if it is being done or not. The law, on the other hand, must be blind and must be equal. So, me being a Judge means I cannot let things go one way to long without being equal, bringing the law back the other way, into balance."

Abbott thought a bit, "So, when one side of the scale has gotten too much from the law, you have to bring the law to the other side to make it even."

"Yes, it's one of my roles in all this. To bring the law equal to everyone. I ain't blind like the lady with the scale. I can see. So I do it the way I want. But I cannot wait forever. Things cannot go one way for too long without going the other. I make the best choices I can. But I got to keep the scale balanced," Stone said and looked tired of the subject.

"Sure," Abbott said, "I got it all but one thing. When you say you are balancing things. I don't know what the two side are," He did not understand and to him it sounded like Stone was talking in circles even though he was clearly trying to make a point Abbott could understand.

Stone looked at Abbott for a bit and then smiled, ending the conversation, "That's mighty insightful Jack."

Abbott let the conversation end as the town of Blackhawk came into full view as they wound around a bend. Blackhawk was the lower of the 'Four Towns'. It stood at eight thousand five hundred feet elevation. Each town was within walking distance of the next, but to walk all the way from Blackhawk the lowest town to Nevadaville the highest would take about two hours, a little less on horseback. Nevadaville was a full thousand feet higher.

Between Blackhawk and Nevadaville were two other towns, Mountain City and Central City. Each town had grown out of its share of the gold rush process. In Central City the mines were worked. In Mountain City the raw ore was stored then transported for refinement. In Blackhawk, the ore was refined and shipped down to Denver City.

At the top, Nevadaville, was the entertainment center. The nature of the gold rush meant Nevadaville attracted all kinds of travelers. Stone and Abbott were not looking for all kinds, but the kind they were looking for was certainly there.

They made their way up the single street that connected all the towns. By dusk they reached Nevadaville. While they were only eighteen miles from Denver City, the elevation and mountains made it feel a world away.

It was getting cold in the high elevation.

They stabled their horses and got two rooms at the El- more Rose. The Rose, as it was known locally, was a two- story building with rooms on the second floor and gam- bling on the first floor. After getting settled they met and together they left the hotel and headed west down main street.

There was only one street as the south side of town was built on a cliff overlooking dozens of mines. The north side was a steep hill leading up the mountain. There were no churches, those were in Central City and Mountain City, where the families lived.

They walked past a couple of decent looking establish- ments until they hit the end of the row. At the end was a big run down looking one story wood structure that was showing its poor construction and years.

Painted on the side of the building was 'Mala Comida'. It could be meant as the name of the place. It could be a warning.

"I think that's Spanish for stomachache," said Abbott.

"Close enough," Stone said as the two men entered.

The inside of Mala Comida was lit by a lot of candles. Someone was playing a piano kind of soft. The music was not your normal knee slapping bang it out but a method- ical ballad type. There were twenty or so people inside. It was about half full. There were conversations going on. The place was not loud, and it was not quiet.

Stone walked up to the bar where a big half-breed Mexican rubbed a dirty cloth around the inside of a dirty glass. He was a good foot taller than the next person in the room. He was probably 300 pounds, but not fat, missing his top front two teeth.

Abbott stood near Stone but positioned so between the two of them they could see the whole room.

"We're hiring," Stone said to the barman, "any suggestions?"

"Picky?" the barman said with no interruption to his rubbing of his glass.

"Sure," Stone made eye contact.

"You're that Judge, ain't you?" the barman said, recognition flashing across his face.

"I believe currently I'm a patron," Stone said with a thin smile.

"My brother had a trial last year down in Deerfield. I remember. You were the judge. I was there in case he got off. He got a real fair shake," the barman held eye contact for a bit, then looked down. Returning focus to the glass. Most people could not have held eye contact for as long as he did with Stone.

"We're bringing Alvord Burton in," Stone said using his real serious voice that carried a room and cut hard. He did not talk loudly but everyone heard him fine.

The piano stopped and the room got quiet.

Stone turned to address the entire room. "Pay is good."

The room was quiet still longer and it was hard to read exactly what people were thinking. The quiet held just a moment longer than either Stone or Abbott expected it to be and they began to wonder if there was going to be a problem, then all at once all twenty people volunteered at the same time.

"I guess we'll be hold 'n interviews then," said Abbott to nobody.

Stone and Abbott used one of the back rooms to talk to potential hires. They were surprised at the number of people that despise Alvord Burton.

There were several good choices, and some odd characters. They mutually agreed that the Rider sisters were the best fit. The sisters always worked together, and Abbott knew them from some work in New Mexico a few years back.

Ruby and Ruth Rider were twins and had a good reputation as trackers. It was not all that common for women to take up the professions, although there were a few here and there. They tended to be mean as spit and very vengeful.

There was one tense moment in their interview, but it passed without much notice.

"You all got the payment money on you?" Ruth had asked during their discussions. Ruby had taken up a position near a window.

"Ruby?" Abbott had asked.

"Ruth."

"Right. Ruth, we ain't exactly suicidal," Abbott had replied. "We ain't going to walk into a saloon full of gun hands with five hundred dollars in our pockets. You will be getting a marker from the Judge here and you can cash it in with a fella named Dutch Levine in Denver City once complete. He ain't hard to find."

After all the terms were agreed to and the sisters left, Abbott had remarked, "They ain't the easiest pair on the eyes those two."

"How do you tell them apart?" Stone had inquired.

"Damned if I could ever get it completely straight," Abbott had said. "but I am near certain they change it up as it pleases them."

THE ARYANA

B y the next morning word had gotten out that Judge Stone was in town. A large group of people gathered outside the Elmore Rose hotel as the sun came up. About an hour after sunup at six thirty in the morning there was a knock on Stone's door. It woke him from a sound sleep.

When Stone opened his door, a small old woman wearing what looked like a circus ringmasters outfit stood in the door frame. Behind her stood a large bald man. The woman spoke with a surprisingly deep voice, "You the judge?" she asked Stone, looking up at him. She took her hat off and held it in her hands as a sign of respect.

"Yes," Stone said. It often happened this way when he traveled. Word would spread that he was in town and people would come to him to settle disputes, for advice, and for other legal matters.

"You got a fee for private work?" the woman asked. Her voice had a hard to place European accent.

"Yes," Stone said.

The woman continued, "We need an impartial are-a-bit?" the woman struggled with the last word and looked up to the large man behind her.

"Arbitrator," the man said softly in perfect English to the woman smiling at her.

"Arbitrator," the small woman said back to Stone as though he was not standing right there and did not hear the short exchange himself, "sorry English is my second tongue."

"You speak excellent English ma'am," Stone said, "my fee is breakfast. I will meet you at the Mala Comida in about an hour."

An hour later Stone entered Mala Comida followed by Jack Abbott. The same barman from the night before was behind the same bar. He was rubbing what looked like the same dirty glass with the same dirty cloth.

When he saw Stone enter he smiled a big smile, "You're good for business friend," he said and gestured to the back of the large room. The crowd from in front of the hotel was now gathered there. They had arranged the room to resemble a courtroom.

There was a table all the way in the back. Presumably for Stone. Then two tables in front of that with several people already seated at either. The rest of the group was seated and standing several feet away from the setup. There were maybe thirty-five people total. A larger crowd than the night before.

Stone started to walk to the back of the room, then paused. Curious he asked the barman, "How did the trial with your brother turn out?"

"You hanged him," the barman said casually.

Stone was surprised at the answer. He did not order the hanging of too many people. Then he remembered, "Your name is Zorito," Stone said seeing the resemblance.

"Yes, it's all good," the big man said sincerely, "he deserved it and the trial was fair. He was a bad dude."

A bad dude was right. Stone thought back to the trial. Zorito's older brother, Jezito, had attempted to extort the small farming community of Deerfield. He had burned, murdered, raped, and terrorized the area for seven months until the town marshal finally hired two gunfighters to help him arrest Jezito and his men. Nearly twenty people lost their lives over the course of the events. Others had their lives, or livelihoods, ruined.

Jezito showed no remorse at the trial and vowed to come back and finish what he had started. Stone had seen no other option than capital punishment. After the memory he nodded understanding to Zorito and, tipping his hat, moved on to the back of the room walking past everyone to his table. On it was a plate with two trail biscuits and a bowl with what looked like strawberry jam, "Thank you for breakfast," Stone said speaking formally to the room while placing his hat on the table to the left of the plate.

He gestured to Abbott, "This here is Jack Abbott my foreman. He is gonna need breakfast also."

Stone sat down and broke one of the biscuits apart, the inside was still slightly warm. He dipped it in the strawberry jam and took a bite. The jam was good, and the biscuit better than it had a right to be. Stone must have made an approving face because he saw the barman Zorito in the back smile to himself as he brought a plate out for Abbott.

Stone finished the first biscuit and pushed the plate to the side. He looked over to Abbott to suggest he do the same. Then speaking professionally, "What is the item please."

The group in front of him looked like European gypsies. He knew some of their customs and knew they would respect him taking fifty percent of his payment up front and waiting for the rest until after the work was concluded.

The large man that had been at the hotel room door stood up from the crowd and spoke, "Thank you Judge for hearing our dispute. We are embarrassed for the need to come to an Aryana. An outsider. But we have no other means in this matter. When we heard who you were, we decided you could help. We are all a single Kumpanias. Do you know this word?"

"Yes, it means you are all one large extended family. Not family by relations. Family by association. It is close to our word, companions. Companions means close to the same thing but without the deep binding implications of your word," Stone said.

"Yes, that is correct," the large man spoke excellent English but spoke slowly so those in the room that did not speak English as well could follow. "We are three Vitsas. I am sorry to question again. Do you know this word also?"

"Yes. It means there are three families by relation in your group of companions," Stone said.

"Ok exceptionally good. Mardas, I turn over to you."

Apparently Mardas was the smaller woman who had come to the hotel. She stood up from one of the tables in front of Stone.

"Judge sir," she began, "My name is Mother Mardas. I am the elder of the Hedji Vistas. My daughter Naome was betrothed to Kennick Nuri. Son of Ringgold Nuri, of the Nuri Vistas," she gestured to the large man who spoke before her to indicate he was Ringgold Nuri.

"Naome was killed two weeks ago returning from a trip. Killed in a rockslide. We have mourned for ten days," she was silent for a moment and many individuals in the room made prayer and crossed themselves. "Naome's younger sister Syeira, who is fourteen, wishes to take up her place and wed Kennick. This would require waiting two years. Until she is acceptable in ages," Mardas pause then continued.

"This is my right and I pass it to her. However, the Nuri Vistas does not want to wait. Bellue Rosella from Rosella Vistas is seventeen. She is the elder of the Rosella Vistas through much tragedy. She has argued her right to wed Kennick. She has historical precedence, some would say, going back to the old country. We would normally have a meeting of elders and decide. However, Ringgold and I disagree and by tradition since Bellue is an elder she cannot be the decider because it involves her marriage."

The room was noticeably quiet and had an air of seriousness.

Marriages came with political implications and other cultural considerations. Stone knew something of gypsy customs, but he had little insights into the deeper social nuances. It felt like there was some undertow here. All eyes were on him when he spoke addressing Mother Mardas, "I take it convening a jury to hear and decide this is not possible due to already established opinions?"

"Yes. Among other reasons Judge," Mardas said evenly.

"What are the counter positions then?" Stone asked.

Ringgold stepped forward and another young woman, presumably Bellue, also took a step forward.

Bellue spoke next.

She was attractive if on the heavy side, "Judge sir. I want you to know that I do not agree with us going to an Aryana. But I have agreed to be bound by this process because I have been told you are wise and fair," Bellue spoke with the same slow perfect English as Ringgold. Given her age it was entirely possible she had been born in America.

"Mother Mardas is afraid if I marry into the Nuri Vistas, she will lose her influence. Then there will only be two families and not three in our Kumpanias." It was presented as a plain truth and an attempt to cut to the heart of the matter. Practical talk.

Stone thought briefly and realized he needed to get to the edges of the considerations as the middle would not provide any insights, "Where is Kennick?" he asked the room in general.

"Here sir," Kennick was a tall kid that looked like his father Ringgold.

"What's your say in all this," Stone asked.

"Naome and I had been planning on being married. For as long as I can remember. I miss her. I feel bad I was not there to help when the rocks fell," he was not choked up, but the words were sadly spoken, and you could feel his pain.

Mardas showed no outward emotions but tears started to fall from the corner of her eyes. She remained stoic and made no attempt to wipe them away or even acknowledge they were there.

Both Ringgold and Bellue looked at the floor. There was a lot of sadness in the room. Stone noticed that there were none of the dancing evil shadows like he had seen at Alamosa. This usually meant that there was no deceit. That things were plain. No intrigue or mayhem for the shadows to enjoy. They liked sadness but it was not enough for them to appear. They sought for self-inflicted pain and physical conflict. Physical destruction.

Stone had a moment of clarity and understood the problem and solution. He could almost see the way through like a visible puzzle, "How long have you lived here in Nevadaville?"

There was a stir in the room from the unexpected question. Feeling it, Kennick looked around. He answered, not entirely comfortable speaking for the group, "We have been here for the past eight years, since they found gold," he said.

"Elders," Stone addressed the three identified elders, "as you mentioned I am an Aryana. I do not know your Romaniya, your laws and customs," Stone gave a thin smile and paused just for a moment before continuing, "however, this matter does not seem complicated to me. I do have one question. It is an important question. I want you to consider it before providing an answer."

The room was perfectly silent and there was weight in the air. A combination of gravity, anticipation, and curiosity.

Stone looked at the three leaders. When he had held everyone's attention for a few moments, he spoke clearly, slowly, and formally, "When do you plan on breaking camp to move on?"

The silence grew very loud and many of the gypsies looked to each other after a short time with a questioning gaze.

Mother Mardas thought deeply.

Some people seemed to grasp a new concept; others just seemed confused.

Mardas finally spoke before anyone else, "We have not discussed that Judge," she looked up to Ringgold, "so, currently, there are no plans to leave."

Stone let the statement sink in until everyone had the chance to hear it and think about it before he spoke again, then asked, "Ringgold is this true?"

Ringgold thought for a moment in the same way Mardas had. He returned her look before speaking, looking at her not Stone when he spoke, "Yes, it is true. We have been here for eight years and have no plans to move on. We have not even discussed the matter for several years."

Many in the room were whispering amongst themselves. Apparently, they understood the meaning of this answer.

Stone looked at Bellue, "Bellue, is this true?"

Bellue did not go through the same level of contemplation that Mardas and Ringgold had. She did not understand the murmurs, "Yes, it is true. What of it?"

Mardas and Ringgold, still looking at each other, seemed to come to a mutual unspoken conclusion. They both were sad. Also relieved. It was something they had not acknowledged but hearing it spoken brought them both to an obvious realization.

Bellue noticed this and looked from one to the other, "What? What is it? I don't understand," she said confused. She was becoming visibly upset.

Stone looked at the three elders as a group, "As an Aryana this is the only solution I can offer you," he said, "I do believe however it is its own truth."

The room was growing louder, Ringgold spoke up, "Mardas and I understand. We will explain it to Bellue and the others. Thank you Judge you are as wise as we had hoped."

"What are you talking about? Nothing has been settled. We haven't even started to discuss this," Bellue was now agitated and her eyes were wide and dancing around in confusion.

"Go Judge, we will explain it," Ringgold reaching out and putting his large hand on Bellue to help calm her, "This is a sad day. Mardas and I will explain it to our companions," Ringgold said using the English word for the first time. He began to speak quietly to Bellue.

The meeting did not so much end as dissolve away into

many small discussions.

Stone put his second biscuit in his pocket. As he and Abbott moved to leave the building Ringgold began talking louder to the group that was gathered, consolidating the conversations, and acting as the leader.

Once Stone was out of earshot near the main door, he noticed that Mother Mardas had followed him. She seemed comfortable allowing Ringgold to talk for her to the group. Stone turned to face her and was met with a serious look on her face. He told Abbott to go on and that he would catch up, which Abbott did.

Mardas waited to speak until after Abbott had left, "You Know?".

"Yes," Stone said with his deep bass of a voice.

She showed no surprise, "The one attached to you, she's no good," looking for a reaction from him.

"I know that," Stone said in a sad tone looking down at her.

Mardas thought for a moment and returned the melancholy smile looking from the back of the room to the front, "We know many of the same things then. I can help. Gypsies have ways," the next part spoken even more sadly, "mountain folk have ways too I guess."

Stone agreed in part, "I appreciate that but my lot in all this is to see it through. It is a deal I made a long time ago," he said.

Mardas became firm, "Spirits are always bad. No good will come from it. They are not all evil. But they are all bad. Bad for you. Bad for themselves. Bad for everyone"

"No good will come from it," Stone replied, "I know it."

Reaching up and putting her hand on his arm in what was probably an effort to console him, Mardas removed the hand quickly showing a quick flash of shock across her face, "You have other secrets," she said coldly, any moment of warmth between them was gone.

Stone's deep bass voice echoed hard, "We all have secrets," there was more of an edge to it than he had intended.

"The spirits are not what they seem," Mardas was not angry, and not earnest, but she was speaking very deliberately now to Stone, "they lie. They are shapes of something we cannot understand. Not completely. They fan the flames that cast the shadows, but they are not them."

"You can see the shadows?" Stone asked her legitimately surprised. He had never met anyone who knew about them, much less could see them, besides himself.

"Yes, some. Not as well as you," Mardas looked down at her hand again.

Stone confessed to her, hoping for clarity, "I see them around people that act counter to things. I see them mostly with bad people, but not always. Sometimes the worst people have none. And people I think are good have many."

Mardas gestured to Stone to lower his head so she could speak softly to him. As if conveying a secret when she spoke next, "Those who know often don't understand. They think they know but they do not. The shadows are the smalls. The between. They are brought about by the little acts. The little sins. Not the big ones."

Stone could smell the rottenness of her teeth. She smelled like an old lady, but continued passionately, "The most evil of people might do huge acts a violence. Huge acts of malice. Cause great suffering. But can be virtuous in their daily lives. They sin big but not small. The shadows have no interest in them.

"A good person may do large acts of kindness, help the poor, donate time and money. But be petty in their dealings. Cheat when counting the numbers. Take more than their share. The shadows will cling to them and dance about them for a thousand lifetimes.

"It can go the other way too. The shadows tell you about a person, but not what you think it means," she concluded.

Stone looked back to the gathering of people, "There were no shadows here today," he turned back to face Mardas, "I took it to mean you were good people."

She released him and looked at him as he stood back up, then smiled, "we are good people Judge. Good in the bigs and good in the smalls," spreading her arms to make the point.

She continued, "But spirits, Judge. They ain't so simple. They dance in the fires for their own reasons. The shadows are what they are, and we can know what they are. But the spirits, they take the forms of things we know. People we remember. But it is not the ones we remember. The shadows tell the truth. The spirits lie.

"The spirits use us. Use our memories. Use our feelings. They do it to get us to trust them.

"So they can get from us what they want from us."

Stone stood looking at her. He knew about spirits. Had deep experiences. He believed her about the shadows. Somehow, he felt he could tell. It made the deal he had made come into clarity. Make more sense.

Mardas was still talking, "The spirits take the form of something we know. Something that will hold sway over us. Here in the real. But they are not those things. They are not those people. They are not those souls.

"They are a mockery of 'm. An outline. An outline of the person held in the flames. The spirits are not just tormenting us. They are tormenting the person whose image they cast.

"They can't hold a form in our world without the original in the flames in theirs. Trapped in their world. Even souls can burn bright as day in the other. For a while anyway.

"The longer you let a spirit go on in our world, the longer the real soul is in torment in their dark world. And the longer it goes on, the more confused we become. We lose what is right and what is wrong. What is true and what is false.

"They study us and become a dark mirror. Repeating our hopes. But backwards like a reflection. They confuse our sense of right and wrong. They distort things. Tell falsehoods. Make us think up is down. Make us think the smalls are the bigs. The between is the real. That injustice and justice is the same."

"How do you know any of this?" Stone asked, amazed at

the information.

"Because the living is the measure Judge, not the dead. It is the living that decides what is and what ain't. Not them.

"They want you to believe that they exist. The same way we exist. That 'is' and 'ain't' are the same thing at the same time when they say it is.

"That what they say is true even when you know first-hand it ain't.

"They want to cast doubt and control you. Influence what gets done. Make it wrong even when you are do 'n right," Mardas held Stone's eyes for a long time in the silence.

Stone was going to speak when the noise from the back of the room suddenly flooded over both he and Mardas breaking the spell. The noise had been there the whole time getting louder but neither Stone nor Mardas had heard it.

Mardas said to Stone as she turned to walk back, "I better get back there and help Ringgold, sounds like what's left of us are not taken kindly to finding out we're just plain old mountain folk and ain't Gypsies no more."

Judge Stone watched her walk away. Maggie was there behind him, just a voice, and said "You know none of that is true Judge."

"I know Maggie," Stone walked outside and headed back to the hotel, "you know I know the actual truth. I seen it. Sometimes I wonder why you all put such effort into convoluting this know 'n that."

THE BIG SLEEP

S tone, Abbott, and the Rider sisters rode out an hour before sunup the next morning.

They were heading west and south along the mountain trail. The day was going to be another cloudless scorcher. As the sun came up mist started to show in the air. The morning dew was being burned off the ground as the sun's rays hit it. Little pockets of steam created a brief few minutes of humidity before it was all gone.

They had to ride through Central City and Mountain City on their way out of the area. The mining process would not be called friendly to the surrounding landscape and the local mountains showed it. Above the towns in the hills were mine shafts. Mine shafts dotted the landscape for as far as you could see. The Colorado territory had fallen into a gold rush several years ago. They called it the Pike's Peak gold rush, but Pikes Peak was over a hundred miles to the south of Central City. They called Central City the richest square mile on earth.

To get to the gold horizontal shafts were dug into the mountains. Gold ran vertical. The general strategy was to use the horizontal shafts as exploratory work and then upon hitting a gold vein to dig down and mine it out.

All that dirt had to go somewhere. You needed lumber for mine support and excavation. What ended up happening was that huge piles of what the miners called overburden ended up everywhere. It was just a lot of dirt but between that and the loss of foliage the landscape looked alien and hostile.

Used up.

Worn out.

Mean even.

Overburden was a good term too. Solid. It referred to the burden of working through unwanted material to get to the economically beneficial stuff.

The mines slowly faded from the landscape as the small group headed away from the four towns. It was going to be about a week ride to get to and cross the Sangre de Cristo Mountains. They were some of the highest in the Rockies having elevations near eleven thousand feet. At high elevations, even in the heart of summer, you could have flash blizzards. Snowstorms.

The plan was to cross the continental divide and then work their way down the west side of the ranges. Once there to go through several of the towns on the western slope and pick-up word of Burton. Heading generally towards the Ute reservation until a more tangible trail presented itself.

The Rider sisters wore cowboy clothes. Each carried a

single Colt Peacemaker on their right hip. They wore blue jeans. Crossed bandoliers on top. Both wore hats in the Mexican style even though neither looked the least bit Mexican. Probably for the wide round brim to shade from the sun.

Stone rode in the front and rode alone. It would take several days of riding along well traveled trails before heading into the wilderness. Ruby and Ruth rode along with Jack Abbott. After a few hours of getting going and not much conversation Ruby finally asked Abbott what had been on both the sisters minds. Because they were a curious sort. Abbott would call it nosy.

"So, I don't understand. What happened with the Gypsies," Ruby said, both she and Ruth were interested and looking at Abbott hopeful. Conversation was an easy way to pass the time.

Abbott looked at them both and smiled the same sad smile Stone had used before, "They were trying to solve a twenty-foot problem with a fifty-foot rope," he said perhaps not as seriously as he could be given the topic. Abbott did not take serious things serious sometimes.

"Could you be a bit more specific," Ruby asked wrinkling her nose and looking mostly at Ruth.

Abbott thought for a bit on how to explain it, "See, they were trying to solve one kind of problem with rules for something else," he said hopefully. Abbott enjoyed talking but he did not always enjoy having to repeat himself in different ways.

He saw they were still unclear, so he tried to be more specific.

"They were not gypsies anymore. They were still using gypsy customs about marriage and how to make decisions. Their group had grown small and they were not traveling any longer," he looked at them both and now they both had their noses crinkled.

"They had settled down," he said as though it was obvious.

Nothing.

Abbott thought a bit longer on how to phrase this so a cowboy could understand, "The Judge gave them a way out by using a different set of rules from a different system," Abbott finally said after much thought and internal deliberation about how to phrase the solution.

The tension left the air, "Sure, the extra rope just tangles things up, it is more than you need," Ruth said to Ruby wavering her arm.

"So, the Judge gave them a loophole," Ruby said back to Ruth who nodded.

They rode on for a while longer and Judge Stone got far out in front. Out of earshot. They were on a well-traveled path just past Idaho Springs. The path was turning more southward and they would ride past people walking or on horseback. Travelers heading up to Nevadaville or one of the other towns who would nod or tip their hats mutually as they passed each other from time to time.

Once Stone was fully out of earshot and the other conversation had faded away Ruth finally asked Abbott, "So how do you know the Judge?"

"We go all the way back," Abbott said. That term was

something Stone and his small group of friends had decided upon as a way of explaining their relationship. "I was a supply sergeant. He was my commander in sixty-four. We were in Meade's Army of the Potomac. First brigade. Fifth infantry."

Abbott paused, reflecting on things. He looked forward and saw the back of Stone a few hundred yards in front of them.

"First brigade under Meade in sixty-four?" Ruby said, thinking for a second and realized what this meant, "first attempt at a siege of Richmond?"

Abbott gave her a thin smile and slight nod.

"Holy hell, that whole brigade was captured by Johnny. Andersonville afterwards?" Ruth said, stunned.

Abbott let his expression change and the smile fade, then another slight nod.

"All this time we know 'n you and you never mentioned this?" Ruth said to Abbott.

Abbott did not tell this story often, although he had told it enough times to know how it went. He decided the two sisters ought to know the history. They were not strangers and he knew them well enough to generally trust them. Or at least be able to predict their behaviors when they all had a common interest if trust was not the right word.

Abbott began the story, "There were only four of us from the Fifth out of six hundred that survived both Richmond and Andersonville," Abbott went on. Not necessarily somber or serious, but not his usual excitable self either, "Myself. The Judge. A fella named Dutch who is holding that voucher in Denver City for you. Another fella named Ned who is currently the Colorado Territory Marshall."

"How did you get captured? I know what was left of the Union army retreated after the first attempt at the siege," Ruth asked, genuinely curious.

"General Grant wanted to drive directly through the heart of Virginia and storm the Confederate Capital. He wanted to end the war and stop the kill 'n. He could have burned the whole state down, he had the time and resources. Many people forget that. They just see what happened. Grant drove three corps within reach. That is over a hundred thousand men. He pushed us hard to get there under forced march for days.

"Supply lines be damned. I had a hell of a time overseeing supplies for the Fifth. Men got to eat.

"We reached Cold Harbor and was worn out bad. We had only a few hours to rest. No sleep. You start twitching when you are exhausted and have not slept for days. I do not think that had much to do with it though.

"Grant launched a massive frontal attack. Even though the damn 'rebs were dug in like ticks on a big fat hound dog.

"He sent wave after wave. Losing one man in four. After six or seven hours it was clear it was over. Men, and these were good men, can only be pushed so far. But Grant was furious. He raged and yelled and demanded we keep charging.

"He settled for one last charge even though it was hopeless. I think he did it to prove he was in charge. That he did not succumb to subordinate suggestions. It was arrogance.

"He was in a fury but there was no one left to lead the charge

"Finally, to order a final charge he demanded volunteers.

"Something a General never does.

"A general does not ask he tells.

"No one volunteered.

"Not from cowardice. From exhaustion. Wounds.

"So, Stone volunteered. He knew not to do it but there was some sense of support for General Grant. A friendship. Something. I do not know the details and the Judge has never shared them. Whatever it was it compelled him not to let the man lose control of his army.

"Stone was shot up. Looked like hell.

"Had been awake for more 'n two days. But the Judge do not retreat. It was clear that was coming next. Retreat and Grant having to admit he lost the men. Lost his command," Abbott said showing no emotion.

"Worked out a soldier in Stone's company got the chance to make the same choice.

"Duty or self. And just like Stone to Grant, we all felt something to Stone that meant we did not want to let him down.

"Just so happened to work out I did not retreat either. Many people learned something about themselves that day. I learned I was loyal and braver than I thought."

It had been a devastating and decisive defeat for the Union and resulted in a chaotic retreat anyway and a later bloody nine-month siege of Richmond to finally end the war. Over forty-six thousand soldiers were killed, wounded, or captured in that single day. The captured ones were marched on to Camp Sumter in Georgia. Also known as Andersonville prison.

It was common knowledge that Andersonville was hell on earth. Many prisoners did not last three months. There was cannibalism, starvation, dysentery, beatings, marshal law, and mob rule inside the walls.

"How did you last in Andersonville?" Ruth knew she was pushing it.

Abbott smiled thinly again.

"Did you escape?"

Abbott's smile faded quick and he was back to not being necessarily somber. He was thinking again. Ruth could not tell if he was reflecting, or choosing his words carefully.

Some time passed.

The hot summer sun beat down on them as they rode casually down the path. There were black birds around. A few more than normal.

"Jack?" Ruth asked.

"Oh, right," Abbott said as if returning his thoughts to the present, "Sure, no me 'n the boys did not escape but it was something like that."

"Something like that? You ain't exactly being the most

specific cowboy on the trail today Jack," Ruby said, looking mostly at Ruth.

"Don't tell us it was another loophole," Ruth said looking from Ruby to Abbott.

"No," Abbott said, "weren't no loopholes there."

Abbot felt they could know; it would help them understand why he was so loyal to Stone he thought. He asked, "You want to hear it?"

"Yes," they both said in turn.

"We studied the situation," Abbott started. He seemed a different man suddenly. His jovial self was completely gone, "there was a big swamp in the middle of the fort. After a while it became so rank you could hardly breathe within fifty feet of it. Maybe a hundred. It was bad, and constant.

"There weren't no choices.

"You break the rules, they would hang you. Had standing gallows. Man got hanged his body would stay until they needed the rope again. Could be an hour, could be a couple days.

"Couldn't tunnel out.

"Some tried. See the ground was soft. Sugar sand in places. Tunnels kept collapsing.

"Hard way to go suffocating underground. Cannot move. You suffocate. Die slow. Every now and then you could hear screaming from under the ground. I think sometimes it was men down there. Sometimes it was not, something else maybe. I do not know. It pulled at your soul hearing it. Tugged at your heart. Constantly.

"You couldn't bribe your way out. They took anything you had long before you got there.

"The camp was poorly built but well designed. There were three sets of perimeters. The first just the dead-line. You go near it and they shoot you from the towers or from the other side of the fence. With no discussion or warnings. Leave the body there for weeks to remind everyone what a fool you were.

"After the deadline you had the fences. They had soldiers in the inner one. Dogs in the outer. It was smart. If I could have gotten to the dogs I may have been tempted to try and kill one to eat it.

"No way to cut through and make it without noise. You cannot bribe a dog when you got nothing. Can't bribe a guard when they got and you don't," Abbott was looking far off, remembering.

"Was not hardly any food either so you were always hungry and tired," Abbott finished.

Ruby and Ruth looked at each other. They knew the stories, most did. They did not know that Abbott was one who could tell it. They stayed quiet and listened.

After he composed himself and took a pause, Abbott continued, "Only people that got to leave were the dead ones. Not the ones from the tunnels or from the deadline. But those that played by the rules and died natural.

"We watched. All we could do.

"Every day the same thing. Round up the dead bodies from overnight. Put them on a cart. Take the cart out of the fort and bury them in a big ditch about half a mile away.

"Day after day.

"They would bring in a hundred new prisoners and take many dead ones. Early on they brought in more than they took out. After a while overcrowding made it hard to stay alive. I believe it reached what they call equilibrium. Same number in and out each day. Or so anyway."

Abbott smiled at the Rider sisters which they took as a chance to ask the question that was on both their minds, "So, you hid with the dead bodies?" Ruth asked in a quiet voice.

Abbott knew the question. It was the same every time he told this tale. Seemed to be a natural conclusion, "No, not exactly."

Abbott continued, "Seems a natural try I agree. Logical. Hide with the dead bodies. But everyone had the same idea. And the guards knew too it was the only way out. Pretty quick they took to poking holes, cutting off parts. Doing things that dissuaded you from that approach.

"They created fear. See that was the real guard. They didn't have to build good fences if you were afraid of 'm. Didn't have to do much. Like I said, it was poorly built but well designed.

"Fear is a funny thing. Especially once it gets into a place. See fear ain't a feeling, it is a disease. Once you catch it, it crawls up into your soul. Turns you around. Justifies doing nothing. If it spreads from a man to a group. Well, the group can do some funny things too.

"Us all being so close it was hard not to catch. Hard to keep away when others caught it bad.

"Stone did not catch it. He seemed to have a natural immunity to it. For him and others. It would leave a person, for a while, when he was around.

"Judge Stone held good rank and had respect. He was able to generally round up enough food for most of us to have a little each day. He would not eat until last. Many days he did not eat nothing.

"Water was the real problem. For some months it rained. Which was good. We could catch water in barrels and cups and what not or just drink it as it came down. Got to wash some too in those months. Then after summer it stopped raining. Which was bad. Real bad.

"Water is heavy. In the months it did not rain much the guards did not bring it too far into the camp.

"Stone would fight his way to where they brought it. Sometimes get some water for us. Sometimes not. The effort, either way, took a lot from him.

"After a while of that, we woke up one morning. He did not get up. You had to go to formation three times a day to be counted. Stone was not there. First time ever. We had not even thought to check on him. He was always up first and helping us. Not the other way around.

"While we stood there, we saw the guards go through the tents and pull out the dead. They carried him out with the others.

"A few days later some of us well enough to walk a few miles were led to a port where they put us on Union ships. Only reason we could walk the ways was because of the food and water he got for us. It was apparently a prisoner exchange," Abbott still had a far-off gaze, "the idea that he missed it by a few days haunted us. Still haunts me."

Ruby felt uncomfortable asking again but she was not getting the references, "I'm sorry Jack, I did not hear you right. How it is the Judge escaped?"

Abbott looked up to where Judge Stone was riding ahead. Stone had stopped and turned his horse around. He was a good way off in the lead. He was looking back and made eye contact with Abbott. Giving him a slight nod letting him know he was OK with Abbott finishing the story.

Abbott turned back to Ruby and it was the first time she noticed how intense his stare could become. He held her gaze until she looked away, "The Judge found us about three months later. We were in an army hospital in Maryland. He says he just woke up in the pit. With all the dead soldiers. Had a puncture wound in his right shoulder. Should have hurt more than it did he said.

"He says the grave was shallow and he did not have to dig much to get out. He just got up and walked away."

Ruth was still confused, "Wait your saying he pretended to be dead and then later found you in a hospital?" she asked.

"No," Abbott stopped his horse and looked at both women so there was no misunderstanding.

"I'm saying he died. The big sleep. Expired. Rode a pale horse."

He looked at them hard and they seemed shaken with the answer. Struggling to believe it even though they knew he was being straight and was telling them the truth.

The three were in the shade of a hill when they stopped. It suddenly went from hot to cold. Even though the breeze had died away. It seemed to be growing darker in the full sunlight. The brighter the light the more everything just seemed like black shadows.

There were a good many back birds around. All quiet just watching the small group.

The blue sky became bluer and a hard line was drawn between the sky and the green hill. The sun was bright yellow but was going nowhere. Its light seemed to dissipate before it hit the ground.

Ruth, Ruby, and Abbott were just black shadows with no other features. Light danced around them but landed on nothing. Stone several hundred feet away was in full daylight, watching.

"You don't just come back from be 'n dead," Ruth said soft. She was looking at Stone off in the distance.

Sound stopped and froze in the air for a long moment. Then suddenly everything returned to normal. There was a sudden rush of air that startled the birds, who all took off together causing a stir in the air. Unexpectedly Abbott smiled, "Aw shucks," he was making both women uncomfortable, "I seen all kinds of things over the years."

He was his old fun-loving self. It was like the story took place in a different world. Now, suddenly, they were back to what they knew, "I can't explain it and don't understand it," Abbott went on, "the Judge has been different too. Kinder, and meaner, at the same time. But he is a man you can count on. He will not ever let you down," Abbott spurred his horse, "ever!" he rode faster than needed to make up time heading towards Stone riding away from the two sisters.

There was little conversation other than necessary communications for the next couple days. Both Ruby and Ruth seemed unsure of how to interact after Abbotts story, so they stuck mostly to themselves. Soon they were off the trails and in the wilderness. As such, they rotated taking point. The others riding single file in no order when not in front.

On the fourth day out, Ruby and Ruth were chatting with each other a bit more than normal when they would trade off point duty. The one not on point would often fall back a few dozen yards for several minutes at a time.

The four had taken to a regular schedule. Up about two hours before dawn. Camp broken down and on the move about an hour before dawn. Stop to water the horses around noon based upon when they would hit a creek or a lake. Make camp at dusk.

After a bit of the solid routine, the four companions had fallen back into normal banter as good trailhands do, Abbott's out of character story past. The landscape had slowly grown barren. It was changing from the northern Rockies that were near Denver City. The colors changing from green to yellow.

They stopped to water the horses near a hot sulfur spring. There was fresh water also about a dozen yards away. You could easily tell the difference because of both the smell and the color of the water.

The big plateau was flat. You could see for a few miles west and south. There were still lots of small slowly rolling swells and several buttes here and there. A butte was a high hill with almost straight sides both down and up. Often buttes had a flat top, sometimes just jaggedly rocks. They were not good for much other than hiding behind or generally getting in the way.

The steam rising from the spring created an other-worldly atmosphere. The sulfur created all kinds of rich colors. Dark oranges, yellows, vibrant blues, and bright vivid greens.

Ruby dismounted and walked her horse over to Stone. He was cleaning mud out of the front hoof of his horse as it drank water from the fresh spring. She and Ruth saw Stone in a different light since Abbotts story. They could not tell how serious Abbott had been but there felt a good amount of truth to it. After hearing the tale, they both noticed that there was a gravity to Stone that you felt when you were around him. It had been there the whole time but now they were aware of it.

"Stay focused on what you're do 'in. Don't look around which will be the natural inclination," Ruby said.

With no sign or shift in his working on the mud, Stone said "Yes I know, we've had a shadow since earlier this morning."

"Yep. I count five riders, although it could be as few as four if they're energetic," Ruby said, spitting and wiping her mouth with the back of her hand, looking down at the ground, being really serious.

"Well, you're better than me I only knew there was that one up there on the ridge behind us," Stone said, finishing up the first hoof and switching over to the second.

"Yep. Huh, I had not noticed him. Good eye," Ruby said to Stone. She very specifically did not look up to the ridge behind them, "well definitely five then not four."

Hearing the conversation from his horse a few feet away Abbott asked, "Any way it's friendly?"

"Only if they are some of the stupidest cowboys I've ever seen," Ruby spitting again, "we moved off the trail two days ago. There ain't no reason to be around here. Or around us. And there ain't no reason for sure to be shadowing a group as dusty as us. Shadowing us ain't called for," Ruby said, looking at her sister Ruth who was a few yards off on the other side of one of the small ponds, studying something.

"Well," Abbott said, "we are pretty far off the beaten path for sure. On purpose. So, we either got some unrelated group thinking we're small fish; or we got us an awfully specific problem."

"Feels specific," Stone said quickly, looking up to the mountain range ahead. The sun was near its apex so his whole face was covered in shadow underneath his Dakota hat.

"Yep," said Ruth, walking across one of the small ponds back towards the others. Water splashing in the half a foot-deep pond. Boots would keep her feet dry but the bottom of her blue jeans were getting wet, "They're either try 'n to commit suicide by cowboy, or they have substantially underestimated their quarry."

"Perplexing," Abbott said, "You know these parts Ruth. If it were me and I wanted to cause us harm, I would circle round that small rise over there about a mile or so north. Staying out of sight. Get in front of us and work up a plan for when we hit the next ridge near nightfall. What about you?"

"Sounds about right," Ruth said.

"So, what are they doing?" Stone interjected in the conversation.

"Well," Ruth said looking in the direction of the small rise that Abbott had pointed out then back to Abbott, "near as I can figure given the way I lost sight of 'm, the rest of them are circling that ridge up there to our north."

"Yep, specific," said Stone, looking northward.

"What do you want to do about that fella on the ridge?" Abbott asked.

"Let's finish watering the horses. He is just look 'n for right now," Stone said, "then let's get some ground between us and him."

WIND

S tone rode his horse hard, as did the three other riders with him.

They had decided to take the initiative. See if they could reach the next ridge of mountains first and lose their potential pursuers. Both those circling around to the north and the single tracker who was about a mile behind them. He would have to spend time getting down the ridge trail into the flat lands which would buy them a large head start.

People often thought the Rocky Mountains were all up and down. Valleys and rivers.

Sure, there was a lot of that. There were a lot of plateaus too. Large open spaces that were relatively, though often not perfectly, flat. Some for dozens of miles at a time. More.

Abbott knew his horses well and knew he could push them for a mile or two at a gallop. After that they would need to slow to a fast trot. If their pursuer wasn't a good tracker, or if he wasn't looking for sign instead working to catch up, this would give Stone and team possibly an hour head start to get to the next range of mountains where they could decide to find ground or continue on at the accelerated pace.

The larger group to the north was a bit more of a gamble. They would also be an additional hour or more behind because of their route through the lowlands. This move could buy them even more time with them.

Stone, Abbott, Ruth, and Ruby slowed their horses to a fast trot side by side after covering about a mile and a half at a gallop, "We should reach the foothills in about three hours," Ruth said, still riding point. "We'll have a couple hours of daylight, maybe a bit less, when we get there."

"Ruby, any way you could get a look at the crew we're dealing with without being spotted?" Stone asked.

"Sure, being sneaky is my specialty," she returned with a smile, happy to have something exciting to do.

Stone then looked over to Abbott, "I've been thinking. I want to change our plan. Jack you and Ruth keep heading south and west. Ruby you try and go get us some useful information. Do not do nothing stupid. Make sure you meet us up at the next ridge well ahead of that group. If you find something out or not," Stone slowed the group down bringing his horse to a stop as he spoke.

"I'm going to figure something out with that fella following us and deal with him one way or another. I don't want to have to deal with all five at once if we can avoid it," his eyes were flat as he drew his sidearm and checked the load, implying what his options may be.

"Judge, why don't I stay here. You go with Ruth," Abbott

said, concerned for Stone and wanting to contribute in equal measures.

"I got this Jack. I'm a better shot than you and a good sight meaner," Stone said to Abbot, spinning his revolver and re-holstering it with a small amount of showmanship.

Abbott started to argue, and Stone cut him off, "Jack you got family. A good life. I'll do it," Stone looked at Abbott seriously and Abbott let the conversation end.

With that Ruby turned her horse northeast, gave it a kick, and rode off.

"Alright Ruth and I will get to the next set of foothills. Once there we will try and figure something out," Abbott said as he turned his horse looking from Stone to Ruth. They rode off heading west.

Stone surveyed the area and decided it would be easiest to just stay here and wait for the ridge rider to show up. Sometimes things needed complicated plans. Sometimes they did not.

There was a strong breeze from the north. The sky was blue. The sun was hot.

Dust blew by from time to time.

Stone kept his view east. Waiting for a sign of the rider. He checked his sidearm load one more time. First the left then the right.

"I didn't like the gypsy lady," the wind said to Stone.

"Now ain't the time Maggie," Stone knew this was going to happen this way. Part of putting up with an attachment was that they tended to take the in between moments away from you. In the long run you grew tired from never having a moment to think for yourself.

"They are a crooked bunch, and they tell lies," the wind said again in a whisper, feigning respect.

"I don't recall them doing much of that yesterday," Stone said. He was getting frustrated with not being able to concentrate on the upcoming confrontation.

"That last bit was all lies," Maggie said from in front of Stone's horse.

"Depends on how you look at it I guess," Stone kept his eye on the eastern horizon, "how about we have this conversation later."

"We all tell lies from time to time, it's the way of things," Maggie said.

"Uh hu," Stone calmed himself. If he let himself get frustrated, he would make a mistake. Or miss something.

"You don't lie Judge. I know. I know a lot. You have secrets but you do not lie about them. You don't tell 'm all. But you don't lie about them either."

"It's true Maggie. But it ain't for no reason other than that is just how I am," Stone checked his side arm loads again.

"I know that too. But it does not matter. It counts the same."

The wind slowed down. Maggie stood there in front of him desperate for him to look at her. She did not say anything for a while.

"Judge, do you think I am still pretty."

What fresh hell. This turn was quicker than most. She was desperate to distract him. Must mean the ridge rider was getting close. He remained silent and observant.

After another bit Stone could feel the breeze on his face. This meant the wind was changing. Now blowing from the east instead of from the north. He could see the dust start to blow up too. He had counted on the cross wind to make dealing with the approaching rider easier. If the wind was shifting this was going to be a lot more dangerous.

"You enjoy the killing Judge. More than you should. More than people think," Maggie remained in front of him. He refused to look down at her. It was possible she now looked like the night she died. Beaten, striped, covered in blood, with a longer than normal neck clawed out at the front. A lot of effort on her part here.

The wind was getting extraordinarily strong now. Pulling at his duster and blowing sand in his face. Maggie was angry and desperate for attention, "What law did McGuire break? What law that required capital punishment?" Maggie was now yelling at him. Her voice getting louder as the wind got stronger.

"They ain't all written down Maggie," finally Stone could see the small dot on the horizon that he knew would be the ridge rider following him. The man was riding fast and would not notice Stone for a few more moments. He would see Stone though. Well before either man was in rifle distance.

With the change in wind Stone changed his strategy. He made sure he was square facing the approaching man to provide the smallest target possible. He would reconfigure his position once he thought he was within range, "Some laws come from man Maggie. Some laws come from God. You know the difference. Just like I do," he said still not looking at her.

The wind, which had picked up considerably, suddenly stopped. Everything was dead still. Quiet. Some dust hung for a second longer in the air and then fell to the ground on the diagonal.

Maggie was gone.

The ridge rider had seen Stone.

He was approaching slowly now several hundred yards away.

Stone waited. Not taking his eyes off the man who eventually stopped and dismounted his horse.

Stone continued to watch as the rider unwrapped a long barrel rifle. He turned his horse sideways. Apparently was going to try and snipe.

This was a tactic taught to calvary soldiers.

Stone continued to watch. With the wind down he was not much worried as the rider had stopped too far away, miscalculating the breeze. While being hit was possible, he knew there were few men, or rifles, around who could make the shot.

The wind started to pick up again and Stone could feel a cold breeze in his face.

Unnatural wind.

He felt disappointment.

"It ain't going to help Maggie. I am better than him. You sure you want this to be the time," Stone said to the air. As soon as he said that last bit, he felt the breeze change direction. It was quickly back to the original warm cross breeze from the north.

The two figures and their horses were silhouetted on the flat plane against the yellow dirt, green mountains, and blue sky.

Stone looked on dispassionately as a bullet hit the ground about twenty feet in front of him and a little to his left. He heard the report of the rifle and could see the ridge rider reloading. That meant a single shot long barrel.

Stone sighed. His horse looked back and up at him and sighed too.

Another shot skipped in. No closer and even farther to his left. In all truth the cross breeze was reducing the odds here considerably. Stone was relieved things went the way they did but did not dare show it.

His horse looked back at him again and sneezed while holding eye contact. Abbott raised good mounts. This one it seemed was loyal but did not like getting shot at. Smart horse.

A third shot rang in. Stone did not hear or see where it landed.

"Ok," he said as he reached back and drew his Winchester rifle.

Another shot bounced in and kicked up dust followed by its report.

"Thank you but still air will quicken this whole thing up," Stone said quietly looking up to the sky and half back over his shoulder.

The air came to complete stillness. Stone aimed and fired in a single motion when the chance was provided. Taking only a second to exhale before he evenly squeezed the trigger.

His shot impacted the ridge riders left leg hitting him hard below the knee. It bent the leg awkwardly taking his feet out from under him and driving his face into the dirt as he slid back several yards. The shot went under the horse, who was startled, bucked, and trotted south a few yards.

Stone spurred his mount forward moving it at a steady pace keeping a close focus on where the rider fell. Without moving his head or changing his focus he ejected the spent shell, reached into his saddle pack, and reloaded the rifle to its full capacity.

As Stone approached within a hundred feet, he could hear the man moaning. As he got closer, he could see the fella looked unconscious and was lying face down, his leg bent at an odd angle below the knee and a lot of blood around him on the sandy dirt.

Just like McGuire. It caught Stone off guard.

The man's rifle, a custom-made sniper rifle, was several yards away after clattering to the ground upon impact.

"Go ahead and roll over," Stone said sounding studied.

The man did not move.

"You don't roll over I'm going to wonder if you really are dead and put a few more holes in you to ease my curiosity," the bass in his voice carried far and had a sense of eventuality in it.

The man believed him and slowly rolled over to go face up. His wounded leg moving gingerly. He had blonde hair in a military style. He was shaven and wore new looking cowboy boots.

Stone had been concerned he was concealing a six shooter under him, but he was not.

"You missed," Stone said looking down from his horse.

"It's a good rifle," the ridge rider said looking up to Stone and holding his gaze, "it's usually pretty accurate from that distance but the wind was doing some funny things just then."

"Mountain weather," Stone said," unpredictable."

"Seems so," the injured figure said as he sat up and studied his leg.

Stone had quick flashes of Alamosa and McGuire again. He tried to shake it off, "How long have you had your horse?" he asked.

The man looked at him squinting with both eyes. Stone was standing with the sun at his back making sure his shadow did not cross the man's face, "Why do you care about that?"

In his black clothing with the sun behind Stone seemed a silhouette. Hard to get a read on. Only his grey eyes seem to catch any light even though the angles made that impossible.

"I'm trying to decide if I shoot the horse, you, or just run it off," Stone said, being honest.

"Mister," the ridge rider said conversationally, "that horse is right ornery and dangerous. The animal is a vengeful bitch. Bit me more than once. If it ain't me, it will be her that hunts you down."

Stone chuckled and the man laughed. It was a genuine moment.

"What unit are you with," Stone asked casually looking away for the first time then back, hoping to take advantage of the pause.

The man smiled, "I'm just a prospector sir," clearly lying and knowing Stone knew he was lying also, "don't know nothing about no units."

Stone got profoundly serious very quickly, "How hard do you want this to go?" He went from cordiality to genuine anger, "for my own reasons I would as soon leave you here than kill you. Mostly to prove something to myself. Some to this damn ghost that is following me around too."

A small expression of concern crossed the fallen riders face. He could deal with mean, had many times. He had not counted on crazy and was not sure what the last comment meant, "Sure, I know. But this only goes one way," exhaling and looking at his leg coming to the realization that it did not matter much as he did not have long. Running his hand through the sand and smiling, "Why don't you just let me go?"

"You going to try and throw sand in my eyes?" Stone said seeing the movement.

"Yep," the man smiled back, "when you come closer," he was a tough fella so this would probably take a while.

"Unfortunate," Stone said to the downed man as he dismounted and walked over closer.

Stone decided to clear the air, "Actions have consequences. You know the choice you made. You elected to fire four shots at me with the intent to kill me. I know you had orders. But there is a difference between legal orders and not so legal orders. And you know which kind these were but followed them anyway," Stone looked down on the man with pity. Unhappy about what had to be done next.

The ridge rider quickly threw sand at Stone and produced a bowie knife from nowhere. The wind picked up into a frenzy. The sun burned bright as time came to a stop in the sudden sandstorm.

It was hard to see exactly what happened.

About half an hour later Stone was wiping his new bowie knife with an oiled cloth he found in the man's saddle pack. Getting the blood off it. He had walked up to the dead riders' mount and spent enough time to go through everything. Eventually taking the saddle and harness off the large animal.

The horse looked at him indifferent and started to walk back north at a leisurely pace. It did not look like such a vengeful animal and Stone was confident he would escape its wrath in both this life and the next.

He had not learned anything from the downed rider, who proved tough as nails. Probably a good man who he would have befriended in other times.

Stone believed him a current member of a special military unit based upon his ability to withstand interrogation and the way he handled himself. Having gathered nothing useful in the process to confirm such a belief. In the end it was just the waste of another good life.

He turned his horse west and kicked it to a fast gallop. Leaving a bloody mess behind him. Feeling pressure to catch up with Abbott and Ruth. Looking to make up as much time as possible.

The landscape quickly returned to normal on what was otherwise a genuinely nice summer afternoon.

SWELL

Abbott and Ruth arrived at the foothills around what was probably five o'clock. There was only one way through the pass. A gorge climb of about five hundred feet elevation over maybe a quarter mile. There were some overhangs. It was a good spot to set up an ambush. It was also an obvious spot to setup an ambush.

Abbott looked back the way they had come, "I reckon we got here first."

Ruth looked up the gorge. Then north. At the ground. Then looked over to Abbott, "Yep we're first."

"Ruby should be here already. We did not handle this as well as we could have," Abbott said to Ruth, "we are too split up. Judge don't normally make tactical errors like this."

"They were good decisions each one. But I agree we ended up suboptimal here," Ruth took her round hat off allowing the chin cord to pull into her neck as the hat hung behind her.

Abbott looked back across the plateau. They had an

exceptionally good view of the surrounding area. They could see far in several directions. When they looked, they did not see any signs of anyone.

"We got maybe two more hours before sunset," Abbott said, "my gut keeps saying not to do the obvious here. Not to head up the gorge."

Ruth looked at him, "Yep I'm hearing the same song. We got to assume the riders we are dealing with are good. We head up there, just the two of us, we will be pretty much committed. With real limited options. Neither you nor I have a rifle. We're both good with pistols but that's close business."

They both looked up the gorge for a few more minutes then Ruth continued, "I think we need to be smart and use this time to our advantage. We should be able to see the larger group now, so something is up," checking the load in her side arm and reaching into her pack, pulling out several more rounds and filling up her two bandoleers.

Abbott walked his horse backward some and started studying the terrain to their south, "Ruth we got no options. I got a suggestion but I do not want to say it. What do you think?"

"I know it Jack. I do not like it but I do appreciate the respect of you letting me say it. We need to ride back and meet up with Stone and hope Ruby is smart enough to double back and find us," Ruth looked Abbot in the eye.

With that they turned and rode in silence for a good bit, both deep in thought. In the rolling plain you could see for several miles when on top of a swell, but only a few hundred feet when at the base of a swell, losing the horizon. They had not seen anyone for several hours then all of a sudden upon rounding the top of a long swell they saw a rider approaching from the east and separately several riders from the north.

The rider from the east was either going to be Judge Stone, or the ridge rider, depending upon which had displaced the other. There would be no way to tell until they were within near shooting distance. Whoever it was, they were at a gallop.

The other group of riders to the north was farther off. They could see them and then would lose them in the gently rolling landscape. Maybe two or three miles away. Not moving fast.

"Spread apart. Let's keep east. It's either Stone or more of the same problem," Abbott said to Ruth and spurred his horse without waiting. He felt confident it would be Judge Stone. The sooner the three were reunited the easier things would be.

Abbott had gotten about thirty yards ahead and met up with Stone after about five minutes of riding. Ruth caught up quick.

"I'm pretty sure their military," Stone said as Ruth stopped her horse, "fella that was up on that ridge following us was well trained. That group approaching is gonna be more of the same. Well-armed and mean."

Ruth looked north, "We got maybe ten minutes. There ain't a lot of options out here."

"Judge you are the only one with a rifle," Abbott said to Stone reminding him.

"Ok," Stone circled his horse. It was still energized from its gallop and was having a hard time with the sudden stop. It didn't want to settle down, "this is not going to go well for anyone. We are looking at a straight shoot out. They count four. I don't know where Ruby is but we have to assume she ain't gonna be part of the next twenty minutes," Stone looked at Ruth who quickly nodded agreement.

Stone continued, "Ruth I want you to take my rifle and my ammo pouch here. Head back up behind us the ground rises some you should get a good view of things. Any shots get fired you open up. Do not shoot at the fellas in front of us unless either Jack or I shoot first, or if you know you are gonna hit 100 percent.

"They will send around a man to circle us. He will see you before you see him. They might send another man around the other way. You see either one, you shoot them. We'll figure the rest out."

Ruth nodded and headed up the small rise with the rifle and ammo bag.

It had gotten on and was around seven in the evening. The sun was starting to set. Falling behind the mountains. If it got dark before this was resolved it was going to be a long night.

Before Stone or Abbott could say anything else five riders rounded the top of the swell to the north, about three hundred feet away. Abbott gasp when he saw that Ruby was the fifth rider. She was beat up bad. Her left eye was swollen shut. One of the men had a rope around her that led from her horse to his horse. There was a lot of blood on her.

The group stopped when they saw Stone and Abbott. "They had not seen us. That is good luck," Stone said to Abbott not taking his eyes off the group. They were talking amongst themselves quickly, surprised. Before Stone or Abbott could speak again, shots rang out. Ruth was firing Stone's rifle as fast as she could. It surprised everyone.

The first shot went wild. The second shot hit one of the riders next to the one holding Ruby's rope square in the chest and he fell backwards. As the third shot was fired the man holding Ruby's rope jumped off his horse, pulling the rope hard that was around her waist. She went backwards and sideways and was out of sight.

By the fourth shot Stone and Abbott had recovered and spurred their horses forward approaching the group of men as fast as they could.

About every second shot was hitting something as the riders scrambled to get off the swell sight line. Two horses were down and three of the men were down and dead as Stone and Abbott made it to the group.

Ruby was a bloody mess. The rope around her had been dropped.

The sun continued its descent and the shadows grew longer.

Ruth appeared running, her horse now several hundred feet away at the other side of the small depression. With her six shooter she started firing into the downed men as she quickly ran over where Ruby was on the ground.

The fourth man had just enough time to get his wits

about him. He had dropped the noose and was able to mount and spur one of his fallen fellows' horses. He mounted the horse fast and took off heading north, wounded but on the run.

The sun went full behind the mountains. The landscape fell into a somber dusk.

Seeing Abbott run over to Ruth and Ruby, Stone pushed his horse and shot off in pursuit of the fourth man, who had about a two-minute head start.

Stone was of modest build with broad shoulders. The fourth man was heavier. Stone believed could push his already winded horse to catch up. Even though the animal was tired.

They raced over flat ground in the fading light. Both horses kicked up dust from the lack of rain.

Every now and then Stone would see a flash. Hear a buzz. He knew this was a pistol fired at him from the rider ahead. After each shot quickly he would hear the report of the side arm right after the flash. He was able to use this to keep pace and know with certainty how far behind he was given the fading light.

As he got nearer to the rider Stone drew his new Remington pistol. Took aim but did not fire. His plan was to shoot the horse and wound the rider so he could get some answers from him. Things had gone so poorly earlier he needed to be careful with this one.

As he thought he was near he realized the gunfire had stopped. The riders' horse was slowing down. Stone slowed also and came alongside the horse and the rider. The man was slumped over. It looked like he had bled out from the original rifle wound as the back of the horse was covered in his blood.

Cautiously, Stone made sure the man was dead. He slowed the horses to a stop and dismounted holding the reigns of both mounts.

Abbott and Ruth were tending to Ruby when Stone returned, riding slow and leading the second horse back to camp with the dead rider atop. He could see from the expression on both Ruth and Abbotts faces that the situation was dire.

Ruby was in bad shape. She was clearly concussed. A good number of ribs were broken. The left side of her face was deeply bruised. Her left eye was swollen closed. She was missing several teeth. Her lip was split and bloody. Her nose bent and broken. The fingers on her right hand, her gun hand, were broken and mangled.

Stone walked over to the dead men. They looked for all the world like soldiers wearing civilian clothes. Their gear, horses, and weapons were military issues. Their hair was cut. They were shaven. He walked back over to where Ruby was, "Can she be moved," he asked, not really a question but a formality.

"Nope," said Abbott, not looking up.

"She gonna make it?" Stone asked, this was a question.

"No odds," said Abbott, this time looking up.

"Ruth your call what do you want to do," not a question, a statement.

Ruth looked up at Stone and held eye contact.

"Next few hours gonna tell the tail," Ruth said as she held Ruby and tried to get her to drink some water.

"Ok," said Stone.

"You can rip up my voucher. I ain't a hired hand no more. It's personal for me now," Ruth said, very businesslike.

"We'll work all that out," Stone said, this time he broke off eye contact first.

It was night now and the temperature was dropping.

"Jack, no fire tonight, we'll cold camp. You let Ruth tend to Ruby. You tend to Ruth. I will inventory these bastards and get the gear off the horses and send them on their way. We just picked up enough weapons and ammunition to start our own militia."

Stone's voice cut through the darkness like rolling thunder.

HARVARD JUNCTION

They waited to break camp until around ten in the morning. Ruby had made it through the night and both Abbott and Ruth believe she was well enough to be moved.

As midday approached it was clouding up, so it was not hot. There was a nice mountain breeze.

They tried pulling Ruby on a makeshift stretcher from some of the materials taken from the downed men. There was too much bouncing around for her own good. Now she rode her horse slumped over and mostly unconscious.

One of the packs Stone had pulled off a horse had a medical bag. In it was some willow bark. He pulled a piece out of the bag and gave it to Ruth to give to Ruby. Willow bark was used as pain relief in the days before aspirin.

They headed south along the edge of the foothills, diverting to a town called Harvard Junction. Harvard Junction had a railroad stop on a run between Salt Lake, Utah and

Wolcott, Colorado. It was not much more than a place for the train to take on water, although there was a working ticket station, a loading dock, and a telegraph had been installed in the train station.

Harvard Junction had been a stop on the Pony Express and looked to have been a good size a few years ago. Currently there was an abandoned post office building, a couple functional buildings, and some small houses for the workers who manned the water tower plus a few other folks who helped support the railroad. There were several abandoned houses and other buildings needed by a larger population but not needed now.

They could see the town laid out before them still several miles away. Stone, who had been on point, slowed his horse and fell back so he could talk to both Abbott and Ruth at the same time, "Ruth, I'm sorry about what happened to your sister. I wanted to find Sheriff Burton and bring him back to Denver City to clear up what happened at Alamosa. I never thought we would be fighting a military combat squad."

There were storm clouds off in the distance and lightning struck far away. The thunder never made it. Stone continued, "Ruth that was good work up there too. Only reason we are here talking about anything is because you acted fast. I know we have got a lot to talk about. There is a fella up here at the junction that I know. We can get Ruby on a train and get her to a hospital, and then we can talk about what we are going to do. I am still formulating and working through things in my head."

As they got closer to the small set of buildings, they could see there was one nicer house among the many present. Stone told them it belonged to the station master and telegraph operator. There were many other abandoned buildings and an empty sheriff's office down the main street

The group stopped at the edge of the main street and Stone headed on alone, walking into the ticket station. In the ticket station was a short man behind the counter. His back was to the door. He was taking dictation from a telegraph machine onto a preprinted sheet of paper. The paper had a series of underline spots in the middle where he was placing letters as it clicked and clacked.

Stone waited for the communication to stop. "Hello Prescott," he said.

Prescott Poole, the telegraph operator, turned unsurprised. He came around the counter and greeted Stone with a handshake.

"Hello Isaac, long time," Prescott said.

"You don't seem rightly surprised to see me," Stone said, his voice low but not thunderous.

"Not in the least. They have been sending a broadcast telegraph over the wires for you. Plus, I saw you on your way up the street," Poole said, pointing to his view of the street outside in a little mirror he kept next to the large machine.

"When is the next train due?" Stone asked, dismissing the other conversation temporarily. Stone was worried about Ruby. He felt responsible for having sent her into danger. He had underestimated the group following them. They all had.

"Train is due in about five hours heading to Salt Lake," Poole said, conversationally.

"Prescott, I need two tickets. We have a woman who has been beaten pretty badly. We need to get her to a doctor in a place with some facilities."

"That won't be a problem Judge, the train is mostly empty," Poole went serious.

"I'll be back in a few minutes," Stone walked out. As he exited, he looked around at the landscape. Going forward he would not make the same mistake again. Here on out he would assume they were being tailed by professionals all the time, seen or not.

Meeting back up with everyone they setup the stretcher and got Ruby on it. Stone and Abbott carried it to the train station. Once there they found a spot inside where they could set it down in a position of relative comfort.

Everything had stabilized and it seemed as though Ruby could make the trip to Salt Lake. She was reasonably aware and interactive. While she could not talk because of the state of her jaw, she could respond to questions fine, drink water, and look around as needed.

They had unbent her fingers last night and got them into splints. Also got her nose back set and generally patched her up. It had involved a good amount of yelling in all directions and her coming and going from being awake or passed out a few times.

Stone refused to engage Poole about the contents of the telegraph, or talk to Abbott about anything, until Ruth and Ruby were loaded onto the train, which had arrived a few minutes early.

They presented their tickets and went through the formalities with the engineer and conductor to get boarded. They had paid for a third-class ticket but as Prescott said the train was mostly empty so the conductor let them use a first-class cabin given the presentation of Ruby and the desire for common decency.

Once everything was set and the train had taken on water from the large water tower on the other side of the tracks everyone said their goodbyes.

"Thanks Judge. I will be seeing 'n you back here day after tomorrow, all things equal," Ruth said.

Abbott said his goodbyes too and he and Stone walked off the train as it began to pull away.

"Well," Abbott said as they watched the train accelerate, "this sure did solve the tell 'n apart dilemma."

Stone looked at Abbott ignoring the comment, "Get me the registration numbers from all that equipment we got off them boys."

Later that night Judge Stone and Jack Abbott were sitting in Prescott Poole's kitchen. The house was modest by Denver City standards, but a luxury for sure out here farther away from civilization.

The room had a large wooden table with four chairs. There was a stove for cooking and heat. The room opened to a sort of sitting area with a few nice comfortable chairs, a red Chinese rug, and two bookcases with a few books between them. The air was a little oily but well-lit with two oil lamps on either side of the downstairs.

It was nice, and warm.

Poole was at the stove making stew. It smelled surprisingly good.

Stone had been thinking since yesterday about things. He realized Maddox had told him point blank that the world had changed but Stone missed the reference. Not knowing of Maddox, he had misread the comment. It was not so much that the world had changed outright but more that Maddox was in the process of changing it.

"Okay Jack. We got ourselves a problem," Stone said, putting down the telegraph transcription papers from Poole.

Stone and Poole were professionals who had worked together both before and after the war. Stone trusted him not to be stupid and was comfortable with him generally.

"The riders back on the plateau, or the telegraph?" Abbott asked.

"Same problem," Stone said. "I didn't want to bring it up with Ruth and Ruby, but that was a military tactical kill squad, no doubt about it now."

"Honestly Judge I think we all have come to that same realization," Abbott said with just a hint of reassurance. He knew Stone was blaming himself for how things went down.

"We were goners," Stone said, "if it hadn't worked out just that way with Ruth on the long rifle, it was over. We got lucky. I was focused on a different problem. Thank god she took the initiative. Even if it was more out of recognition of the situation on her part than any kind of brilliant planning on mine."

"So, it begs the question," Abbott said, "Why would a five-man military kill squad be interested in us. And how did they get organized so quickly and pick up our trail three days in?"

Abbott thought for a second and realized that this was only half of the situation, "What does the telegraph say?"

"It says the military is preparing a retaliatory strike against the Ute. And that my jurisdiction has increased a bit," Stone said.

Poole brought over the stew in bowls and put one each in front of Stone and Abbott, but no one had much of an appetite.

As the night progressed Stone, Abbott, and Poole all sat silent at Poole's kitchen table. The stew got cold and remained untouched. The oil lamps got turned down.

It was getting late.

"James McGuire. Gus Maddox. Prescott, what do you know of them? I cannot figure out how these two pieces are connected, and what they are the start of," Stone said, looking at Poole, "you are out here on the edge with that damned wire service. What is go 'n on that I ain't putting together?"

Poole thought for a second.

"I can give you some common knowledge. I do not normally have conversations last 'n more than a day before someone moves on. But I have a lot of conversations if you know what I mean. I get a picture of things," Poole said, just setting expectations.

"Sure, it might be helpful just to hear it back," Stone said. "Jack, listen close too, we're missing something easy here."

"Well, story is that McGuire was falsely accused of kill 'n folk to get their land deeds," Poole said sheepishly looking down and then up at Stone to make sure he was not getting mad.

"Go on Prescott I want to hear the scuttlebutt. Ain't going to dispute facts with you here or now," Stone said in a comforting voice.

Poole continued, "Okay sure. In the middle of the trial the Ute Indians attacked Alamosa try 'n to kill McGuire since the land he was acquiring was bordered to the north side of their new reservation.

"They killed everyone along with a number of McGuire's company men as he and Sheriff Burton tried to fight off the Indians and save the town. They showed where they held up in an alley and tried to save as many folks as they could, to no avail."

Poole looked back up. Stone was neutral looking, studied.

"There are a couple different variations of it but that's pretty much the gist," Poole said, quietly. "So now they're bringing the army in to rebuild the town. They put this fella named Maddox in charge of both the Colorado military and law enforcement. Most folks are happy about it.

"They say it will make it easier to deal with the Indians,

and with the outlaws. Maddox raised money from Washington D.C. to repair the town and acquire the rest of the land McGuire was trying to get. And as I understand it, several more miles into the Ute territory, for safety reasons given the breach.

"Maddox has been sending his men to most of the larger towns to help the local authorities with peacekeeping. There has been big recruiting for the new militia too."

Abbott interrupted Poole, "Peace keeping, what a thumper!" almost despite himself, "I ain't no Indian lover but I come to terms a while ago. Just like they did. That things are what they are. How can we give 'm a reservation, then send the army in not less than a year later to take it back?"

Everyone was quiet for a bit so Abbott continued, "Besides, there ain't nothing special about that land. I been there many times. Ain't good for grazing. Ain't where they are finding gold. Ain't on the ways to anywhere that the railroad cares about. Cannot grow nothing there. What is Maddox needing money for he ain't buying it back from the Indians he is taking it. Spending on something though."

"Maybe that is it Jack," Stone said, a light going off.

"Maybe what's it?" said Abbott, lost.

"Only way it makes sense," Stone continued. "They found something there that no one knows they want yet. It is not valuable now. But it's gonna be once folks start want 'n it. They figure it's easier to get it now when no one knows they want it."

"You're going in circles a bit Judge," Abbott said, "only

thing on this land we're talk 'n about is a few abandoned unsuccessful homesteaders and a big mud lake. The rest is the northern part of the reservation. It is a lot of nothing. It is bad land. Rocky. Barren really. Once you get farther south it gets okay. Livable. If anything, you would expect them to be trying to take back the southern part. It at least could be farmed."

Poole had been listening to the entire conversation. "You know, I got some other things now that might make sense. I didn't even know I knew until now."

"Let's hear it Prescott now's the time," Abbott said, getting animated at the possible solving of a mystery and agitated at the same time for the complexity of it.

"Well it's just interesting. The Army was already here before they got called to Alamosa. And they got here two full days before their orders came across the wire to get here," Poole said.

"What army?" Stone asked quickly. Finally putting everything together, "this Colorado militia I keep hearing about or an actual Federal regiment?"

"The Colorado militia," Poole said taken back at the energy Stone suddenly exhibited.

Poole finally went to bed near two in the morning. Stone and Abbott were still sitting at the kitchen table. Both were now drinking coffee, and had eaten some of Poole's stew, which was exceptionally good, even cold.

The night was winding down.

Once all other conversations were over, Abbott asked, "So Judge, earlier when we were riding up to Nevadaville we were talking about the lady with the blindfold and scale."

Stone looked Abbott in the eye, "Sure I remember."

"Well. You got pretty ornery with me when I talked about justice instead of the law," Abbott was a little sheepish.

"True I did," Stone said still looking at Abbott.

"Judge I been trying to think on it. I honestly don't understand what it was about that got you going."

"Jack," Stone began, "for me the two things are about as different as night and day. I know you did not mean anything by it. And I know that my view of things ain't everybody's."

"Sure Judge. But I would not mind understanding."

"Alright Jack," Stone pulled deep, he hated this conversation, but Abbott was a good friend, "What is the law Jack? Give me something to start with."

Abbott thought for just a second, "The law is how we are supposed to behave."

Stone showed surprise, "That's a good answer Jack. Let me just say it back to you with a few formalities.

"The law is a system. It is a system of rules. Rules that we as people are able to recognize. Rules that explain generally how we are supposed to behave when around other people.

"There are a few important pieces here.

"The first is people generally being able to understand the fact that there are rules. The second is them being able to associate the rules to the things they do."

"I can see that" said Abbott.

"But then the question becomes. So what?

"What is the cost of following the rules or not following the rules? And who gets to decide what the law is anyway? Who gets to apply a consequence to either following the law or not following the law? Who gets to write the law down. And is it still law if it ain't written down?" Stone paused and looked to Abbott for an answer.

"Well Judge, there is a lot there. Let me start by saying that I do not think it is a law if it ain't written down. Would not be fair," Abbott responded sincerely.

"Really Jack?" Stone looked surprised again, "Where is it written down you got to hold a door for a lady coming out of church?"

"That ain't no law," Abbott responded dismissively.

Stone smiled, "Sure it is. It is a social law, but that is still a law. Look at it this way and you know where I am going. What happens if you don't hold the door and someone sees you? I remember you telling me stories of you growing up and how you were flicking the ears of William Fieldman when you were a boy for that very deed."

"Well, everyone knows you hold a door for a lady. And that lady was my mother!" Abbott exclaimed.

"Fits our definition doesn't it?" Stone drank some of his coffee, "A rule that young William could understand about how he was supposed to act around people. And if your stories are even half true, he suffered dire consequences for it. So, in that case you decided what the law was. You enforced it. None of it was written down any-where."

"That feels tricky Judge."

"Really?" Stone leaned forward, "Okay. How about back with the gypsies just a couple days ago? You agree with how all that went down?"

"Yes," Abbott was not feeling as certain as he did a few moments ago and it came out almost as a question, "I even explained it to Ruby and Ruth. But I now see I did not even know what I was explaining!

"Sure enough Judge. I told them they were using rules from one system to try and solve a problem in another!

"It's just what you said. Even the same dang words.

"How could I know it then but not even understand it?

"I thought I understood it fine. It all made good sense. And I do know it. But I didn't realize I already compre-hended," Abbot said with an introspective look.

"That's okay Jack. This seems simple. It is on some levels. But it is also complicated at the same time. I think we are agreeing to what the law is now. Right?"

"Yes we are agreeing. I get the point. But that do not an-swer nothing," Abbott said the last part almost to him-self a little disappointed.

"We ain't done. I will give you the whole thing. But we got to walk through it from front to back.

"So we now agree on what the law is. We recognize that it is what it has been all along. That the law is a system of rules that are understandable by a person.

"We also just agreed that there are different systems of rules, correct?

"Some written down. Some not. Some made up by a few people. Some made up by almost everyone.

"When you were little and picking on poor William for not holding the door for your mom. How did you get to be a law enforcer? Why were you able to enforce the law? You were just a kid and the law wasn't even written down."

Abbott contemplated the question knowing it was on the way to something else but wanting to give a good answer, "Seems to me I was bigger than William and meaner. And I cared about my mom. So, I could do whatever I wanted with him."

Stone answered quickly, "But you didn't want to do too much with him generally. You just wanted him to treat your mom with respect. When he did not you wanted to make him do it right the next time. To punish him specifically for something he did so that next time it would go within the rules as you believed in them.

"Not just because you could. Not because you even wanted to. You probably did not want to. But because he broke a law. Not a big one. But one important to you at the time."

"I was stronger than him," Abbott said to himself trying to understand his actions when you put it in this context and not overly happy about what the answer might imply.

"You mom wasn't stronger than William. She was sickly.

No offence Jack," Stone said.

"None taken," Abbott said comfortably. Abbott's mother had been a frail woman who died of pneumonia when he was in his early teens.

"William held the door for her from then on. Right?" Stone asked.

"He went out of his way to do it. Yes."

"For your mom, the law protected her even though she was sickly. Matter of fact we could argue because she was sickly. So in this case the law worked for the weaker not the stronger. Just depends on how you look at it."

"Okay Judge. I am seeing your point again. And again, I already knew this but for some reason it seems more complicated when you try and apply these ideas as stuff is happening," Abbott said.

"It all transfers Jack. We are using a simple example of a simple law, hold the door for a lady. Barely a law really but it is one. The core principle here works at all the different levels. This is what I do, and what I mean when I say I got to balance both sides.

"If as a boy you had been more vengeful with William, and got caught, and I was the Judge, I would have to make sure that William got as much from the law as you did. You were right to flick his ears and get him to be respectful to your mom. But had you beat him up, or worse, you would have been wrong. See the law balances things. Like the lady with the scale. But it's got to work for both sides."

The two were silent for a bit then Abbott asked, "So now,

at the risk of suffering your wrath again, why ain't that justice too? It seems the same to me."

Stone internally steadied himself. He hated this topic and could easily grow angry when discussing it, "Jack I'll try and go over this. I got a lot of ropes pulling a lot of direction on this one so try and stay with me."

"I will Judge," Abbott said, genuinely wanting to understand how his friend saw things and knowing Stone to be incredibly wise in this area.

"Let's stick with our simple example of you and William. I know it is kind of silly, but it is so simple we do not pick-up other baggage.

"We talked about that the law is a system of rules that people can understand. Justice is different. In our example, there was no justice being served by you flicking Williams ears. And no justice was served by him letting the door close and bump into your mom and knock her down.

"See, the law looks at actions and reactions, and applies consequences to them. It is a continuum. It encourages people to adopt it.

"But justice is different.

"Justice depends upon where you elect to start thinking on things. It has no balance. It can bend one way and never bend back the other.

"What if for you and William things started when you began flicking his ears and yelling at him?

"What if he decided an eye for an eye and a tooth for a tooth and he wanted justice. He goes and gets an even bigger boy who comes back and beats you down. Him saying it was justified because you were picking on him. For justice sake he had to do a little more to you to make it fair.

"Then you decide you need justice too. Because after all you was just looking out for your mom. Now this bigger kid is beating on you.

"You go get a gun. Just to scare him but it is the only way. You cannot get justice by fighting him he is too big. He is not scared and starts wailing on you again anyway. He is gonna hurt you bad this time. Worse maybe. Justice, you pulled a gun on him and scared him.

"You ain't helpless though, you got the gun. So you shoot him in the leg. Justified right? He was beating you bad. Maybe was gonna beat you so bad things will not work right. Self-defense! Justice!

"His father sees you shoot him and standing over him. He does not know nothing except his boy has been shot. It is all new to him he does not know no history.

"He shoots you dead not knowing if you were gonna stop there. Justice! Protecting his boy!

"Your mom now has lost her only son and you are dead. A boy is shot in the leg might never walk right again. His pa now just killed a child, you.

"But every step of the way, Justice! Self-defense! An eye for an eye!" Stone spoke the whole time working to keep his voice down. The last part was loud. His low bass voice booming in the small house.

Abbott had followed along the whole way and understood each reference, "Sounds like justice and vengeance are pretty close," he said seeing Stone growing tired of the conversation.

"It is worse than that Jack," Stone calmed himself down and knew he owed it to Abbott to finish explaining things.

"You applying the law in our little example, a small law, but a law none the less, to William to act better was appropriate. But it did not bring justice to your mom. There was no justice for how God treated her at the end.

"It had nothing to do with justice. There was not justice in it for you. None for William. None for anyone. It was a matter of law. Social law, to be exact, not legal law, but there is not any difference.

"Using the law everything worked out fine. Good even. William learned a lesson and became a better person. Your mom got more appropriate respect and felt more dignity near the end. You were a good son and people recognized it.

"Justice though. What a mess it would have created. Justice depends upon where you enter the goings on. It is as much about when you start paying attention as anything. If we started the story with you flicking Williams ears instead of him being rude to you mom, he would be due justice not you.

"It could be William had his own story going back further. Maybe his father beat him that morning. Maybe he had been up all night tending to a sick calf and was not thinking straight. Who knows.

"Law do not need to know that, justice does. The law is what is. Justice can be what it ain't. And justice always brings a new beginning.

"Justice asks: What now? What of it? How do I feel about it?

"It is messy work. Open for interpretation. Hard to stop once it starts.

"Had you tried to apply justice as a boy, it is right likely things would have worked out terribly for everyone."

Abbott had been able to follow along and understood the points again. After several moments of silence as he was running through everything in his head, he asked, "Judge I understand. I do and I appreciate you taking the time to explain it to me. I know you had to simplify things. I do have a question though. Are you saying there is no point to justice at all? That it should be avoided?"

The conversations always ended up here.

Stone drank some more of his coffee and got up to refill his cup, "Not at all Jack. I often do point out that it is hard for a person to truly know what justice is. Especially in any given situation.

"But that do not mean it is impossible. You just got to think your way through it. You cannot let your emotions drive you.

"Emotions get justice wrong every time. It is easier to worry about the law. What is legal and not so legal is a safe place. It can be a clear picture. You can know when you are doing right.

"Or not," Stone finished.

They both drank coffee in silence for a time it was getting

on after three AM.

Finally, Stone spoke again, "But to bring things current, and counter pretty much to what I believe and what we just discussed, I am going after Maddox for justice.

"For sending those men after us. For what they have done to Ruby.

"For all those people they murdered at Alamosa a month ago. Each one of those people had their own story Jack. Just like you and William. It is possible to reach a tipping point where justice is the only answer. Where the law ain't enough.

"Even though I got the law on my side on this one. Conspiracy to commit murder with malice of forethought. Theft of private property. Destruction of private property. Intimidating a witness. Attempted murder of federal authorities. Interference in civilian law enforcement," Stone sat back down at the table his coffee cup now full.

"But I ain't doing it for the law. Not now.

"I am too mad. Emotions make justice wrong every time and I am spitting mad Jack.

"As much as I despise it. As much as I know it is wrong. As much as it goes against what I believe and what I agreed to do.

"As much as it is counter to who I am. It is the only choice I have. Today, for Maddox, I am all the justice he deserves."

SEND IT

R uth arrived on the morning train from Salt Lake three days later.

She looked rested and washed. Her report was that Ruby was doing well in a hospital in the city. That she was past any concerns other than just the process of healing, which would take several months.

Stone and Abbott brought her up to speed on their plan and about the situation. They were all sitting in the small train station that had the telegraph office in it which is apparently where Poole spent most of his time.

"So that explains how a military tactical team could be on us so quick. I'm still a little cloudy on the angles as to why," she said.

"We don't know exactly, but we know generally," Abbott said, proud of himself to be able to explain the whole complicated matter to her.

"There is some type of cahoots between the private money associated with the railroad that McGuire was leading up and elements of the Colorado government or at least the Governor and this fella named Maddox who is heading up a Colorado military that is also replacing civilian law enforcement throughout the state," he continued, "or at least some parts of it."

Abbott had to pause to run through it in his head a second time to make sure he had it all.

"Which has led to murder 'n a town full of folk, being willing to send the Colorado army to kill a federal judge including us, and a potential unnecessary war with the Ute. Among other negative yet undiscovered prospects," he finished.

Everyone stared at Ruth to see what she thought and to see if they were able to explain the situation adequately to her.

"Seems kind of dire," she said after thinking on it a bit.

"Seems terrible," Abbott agreed, "these are all some big players. And the whole affair seems organized. What is worse, we just got things all agreed to and peaceful with the Indians and now it looks like that will be destabilized again."

With the explanation finished, Poole looked nervously at Stone, standing next to his telegraph machine. He knew this next part was coming and had been dreading it for the past day.

"I ain't never sent a telegraph like this," Poole said, trying to find a way not to send it.

Abbott and Ruth Rider watched Poole closely after being brought up to speed on the rest of the new plan.

"Send it," Stone said thunderously.

RAIN

Stone, Abbott, and Ruth Rider had walked back to Poole's kitchen. Poole was still at the station at Stone's instruction waiting for a reply from his telegraph.

It was getting dark outside. There was frequent lightning in several directions but still no rain. It smelled like rain was coming.

Ruth on the way back wanted to clear the air with Stone and Abbott, "When we signed on, I thought we would be going after Burton to bring him back to Denver as a witness. I knew it would be hard work, but it did not seem all that dangerous. Seemed appropriate really to help him do the right thing. He is not known as a stand-up lawman by any means."

Stone looked thoughtful, "I agree, it's different than I thought too. I had believed folks were confused and I understood things. But given we just had a military squad try and kill us, and that they were in civilian clothes, I think we have established its something bigger. Putting them in civilian clothes changed things. Opens up into my jurisdiction.

"The goal was never Burton; he was a means to an end. I thought we was working inside a system. I was trying to solve the wrong problem. Using rules from one thing to solve another. Worse almost got us all taken out right here at the start.

"I was naive," Stone concluded matter of fact. It was clear he was hardening some to the players and the situation. Giving up some of his balance, losing patience.

"I don't think believe 'n in the truth is naive Judge," Abbott said, noticing Stone's dark mood.

"We give 'n up?" Rider asked.

"Seems like there's too much on the line to give up," Stone said.

There was a long silence.

"So, I am going to call in a favor. Something I swore to myself I would never do. We must investigate and understand what this Colorado Militia is, and how military men were ordered to come after us.

"We have to stop these fools from rekindling war with the Ute. We have to figure out why that land is so valuable.

"And we have to bring Maddox and his men to justice for what they did to all those people at Alamosa," Stone said forcefully.

"What about Burton?" Rider asked, not stuck on it but curious.

"I would say he is an afterthought at this point. I do not believe he was more than a mid-level operator in all of this. Maddox, to me, seems the point man. After we deal with him, we will need to understand the broader workings here in the Colorado government," Stone said as the lightning outside flashed in the sky, "but either way there ain't no one in Denver City I am interested in trying to convince of anything. Bringing Burton back has lost its purpose."

"Well good thing we brought a lot of ammo," Abbott said, trying unsuccessfully to lighten the mood a bit.

Poole returned a few hours later holding several pages of transcribed telegraph messages for Stone. His hands shook slightly as he handed the papers over. He avoided eye contact with the Judge.

"Good Lord Prescott you look like you have seen a ghost," Abbott said, looking from Poole to the papers to Stone and back.

Stone read the papers. Nodding his head in agreement as he took in each line.

"It's from President Grant," Poole blurted out, trying unsuccessfully to light his pipe in the corner of the kitchen with fire from the stove. It felt forced. Like he had been trying to get that out since he walked into the room.

Abbott and Rider watched Stone, waiting.

"You called in a favor from Ulysses S. Grant?" Rider said, thinking this might be a joke.

"I did," Stone said with no humor, "did you ever wonder how someone becomes a federal judge?" he asked, adopting a patient tone.

"Well, no," said Rider. "I just knew you were one. I never

really thought about how it happened."

"You get appointed by the President," Stone said.

"It's from President Grant," Poole said again, completely out of context, as a sort of reflex after hearing Stone say President.

The three others looked up at Poole from their conversation. He looked kind of unfocused and smiled a thin smile.

Outside lightning struck with immediate thunder startling everyone except Stone, who's eyes seemed to pick up some of the electricity in the air and almost glowed.

All at once it began to rain hard.

Stone explained what the two different telegraphs said which took a few hours of conversation.

After some discussion Abbott asked, "So, you got a new military commission?"

It was the middle of the night and still raining hard. The front of the storm had passed. The lightning and thunder had subsided a good deal.

"No Jack not exactly. I have been appointed as a Special Investigator attached to the War Department. It is a civilian position but it carries the military rank of Major General in matters specifically relating to the investigation. However, since I am now investigating the Colorado militia, well, there is some military overlap.

"This means I have federal authority as a Judge from the Department of Justice and also military authority from the War Department," Stone said, "so like it or not as of now I out rank any possible Colorado militia officer. I have the authority to direct local or federal Army resources however I see fit as there ain't no other Major General within a thousand miles of here. If Maddox really is bringing up his men to take over local law enforcement, I can put a stop to it. I believe in the civilian authority for law enforcement and think mixing it with the military is a bad idea."

Abbott and Rider, and everyone else in the western territories, was accustomed to a simple system of civilian justice. Towns may or may not have a sheriff. Bigger cities like Denver City may have police. Both sheriffs and police got their authority from the town or city council and enforced laws made by the town or city council.

City councils were elected. They had well-defined jurisdictions.

Larger areas like territories may have a marshal, and enforced laws made by the territory within the whole territory including the small towns and larger cities.

The federal government had its own laws. They were enforced by US Marshals or their deputies, across towns, cities, territories, and states. Most places adopted the federal rules as their own and then added to them. In either case laws could be appealed at any level in court, by a judge, broken down in about the same ways.

The system was spotty and locally the names and terms could switch. You could have a town marshal and a county sheriff. The roles were generally consistent, and there was a loosely understood hierarchy to things. Everyone understood the idea of jurisdiction even if it was not always followed to the letter.

The important thing was that, more or less, the system worked.

"President Grant wants men he can trust to look into things for him under special federal authority when it's warranted," Stone said.

"Warranted like a rogue territory militia trying to murder a federal judge and start a war with the Ute?" Rider asked, maybe a half step in front of Abbott following everything.

"Or like that same militia dressing in civilian clothes and killing all the people in Alamosa," Abbott said, catching up quickly.

"Or the army showing up two days before it knows it's supposed to be here," Stone said. "This situation warrants special investigation."

"So, can you arrest people?" Rider asked.

"Not exactly. I can issue a warrant for their arrest, and otherwise force them to comply with my investigation using the full weight and measure of the federal government," Stone clarified for her, "the important thing, I think, is that I can issue legal orders to military units. There is not any confusion when it comes to military chain of command. I now outrank even the territory governor when it comes to issuing military orders."

"Are you still a judge?" Abbott asked.

"Sure, absolutely. But my jurisdiction has been expanded for this matter a good deal. I ain't just doing bench work now though, I think that time is over and it is time for sentencing," Stone said, "but, all that is just paperwork.

Without muscle Washington is a good way off from here. No telegraph or stack of papers is going to carry the day.

"That is the second Telegraph. Some weight for us. We are going to need some federal troops to back us up. Maddox is not going to have any interest in doing what I tell him. And there ain't no piece of paper that will help. He will need persuading," Stone said with a grim look on his face.

It continued raining into the next day. The clouds were low given the elevations. Gray and puffy. Full of water. The lightning seemed over and now it was just the cold wet constant rain.

Everything that had been very dry was now very wet. The principal characteristic of the landscape changed from dirt to mud.

There was mud outside, mud inside, mud on the front porch, mud on your boots, and mud on the horses.

By the end of the day there would be mud in the sleeping mats, on the saddles, and pretty much everywhere else that mattered any.

Stone, Abbott, and Ruth Rider took breakfast with Poole. He was a heck of a cook. After breakfast they saddled up and headed out into the rain.

And mud.

Stone had his collar up and hat down, as did Abbott. Rider had produced rain gear from somewhere and was getting the better of the rain in it.

They rode south and a little west, as the mountain passes would allow. There was not a direct route between Harvard Junction and Alamosa. They generally wanted to stay off any common trails.

Judge Stone rode in the lead, Abbott, and Rider a few yards back. The group stayed together not like before where they would get spread out by as much as a few hundred yards. Before they had assumed friendly territory. Now they had to assume hostile.

Otherwise, they went back to their old routine. Up a few hours before dawn, camp broken down and on the move an hour before sunup. Stop to water the horse's midday. Camp at dusk. The rain became a steady drizzle for the next several days.

The landscape became very mountainous. After the end of the first day, they had ascended above the tree line. This put them higher than eleven thousand feet above sea level. The rain turned to snow. It was cold, but as a summer storm it was not dangerously cold, just uncomfortable given the group was wet and covered in mud from the ride up.

Some of the trails they followed were hardly more than mountain goat paths. They went dangerously close to high drops. The horses were solid but even they struggled from time to time with footing.

To camp at night they had to find overhangs and rock formations that were stable. They could not use caves or other perfect areas to sleep because they tended to already be occupied by wildlife. Some extremely dangerous like bears.

As they made their way over the summit of Harvard Peak they could see hundreds of miles in the distance looking in the direction of Alamosa. To the east of their chosen path was the great Colorado dune sea. Hundreds of square miles of moving sand. A mini desert to be avoided most any time but especially in the summer months. Stone had purposely made sure their path came in west of it.

Over the next two days the landscape changed again as they slowly made their way into the San Luis valley. The valley was at seven thousand feet above sea level and was surrounded on all sides and was still green and lush. It was a hundred miles wide and two hundred miles long from north to south. There were a few cattle farms here and there.

The three riders rounded a final hill and could see Alamosa laid out on the southern end of the big valley beneath them.

The rain had stopped in the morning and the sun was currently out. Things were just starting to dry off.

Clouds of mist hung in the air as the sun shone brightly.

It was becoming a pleasant warm sun, not hot. Coming off the mountain summit it felt fantastic to be back into warmer summer weather.

To the east was an army campsite with nearly fifteen hundred soldiers. There were tents laid out in clean lines.

The military camp was much larger than the town, which was a bustle. Alamosa had new buildings going up along the main street. Formal construction was underway to replace the courthouse and other lost structures.

There was military everywhere. Alamosa almost seemed to be being rebuilt as a military waystation.

As the three rider's rode into town, a work crew noticed

them. The groups approach each other. The four-man crew walking up the main street carrying several large boards, heading to the new courthouse site.

Stone was in the lead and maneuvered his mount to be in their way even though the main street was very wide. The lead soldier, who wore sergeant stripes, looked up at Stone and started to issue a command for him to move but stopped upon recognizing him. A surprised look flashed across his face and he seemed indecisive for just a moment. Then his demeanor changed to be slightly more accommodating.

"Pardon us Judge," the soldier said, showing he planned to go straight through where Stone and his horse were.

"You recognize me son?" Stone asked the man.

"Yessir," the sergeant spoke formally as if to an officer, "we all know who you are. There was a briefing a few days back. But we did not get instructions for talking to you. Just instructions to report seeing you if we did."

"Who is the commander in charge here sergeant?" Stone asked, ignoring the soldier's stance and comment. Stone was looking off to his left, casual, but he spoke in that commanding way.

"General Maddox sir," the sergeant said, "you can find him in the big tent over in our camp."

Stone smiled an ironic smile at the soldier, "Sergeant, is that the same General Maddox who not more than two weeks ago was Colonel Maddox?"

The soldier understood the reference, "Yessir."

Stone was genuinely curious, "How does one go about

needing a General for a territory regiment that ain't really the size of one full battalion?"

A typical infantry regiment was two battalions, about a thousand soldiers. A brigade was more than one regiment, often as many as four. Typically, a colonel ran a regiment, a general a brigade.

The sergeant looked to his work crew companions who each shrugged their shoulders to indicate they didn't see any harm in explaining to Stone what they knew so the sergeant answered, "Yessir. We are now the first Colorado brigade. The General sir has been recruiting a lot of men recently. We've got three regiments now and two new regimental commanders."

This meant the Colorado militia was now at least three times the size of what Stone had observed here in Alamosa as he rode in. Maybe more. Maddox it seemed was busy and had managed to promote himself both literally and figuratively.

"The rest of the men are formed up down south near the Ute reservation," Stone guessed but said it so casual it came out as if he already knew.

"Yessir."

"You gonna report seeing me?" Stone asked.

"Yessir. Got to. Everyone you run into is gonna report seeing you. They were pretty clear about it. Spent extra time on it if you know what I mean."

Stone held eye contact until the soldier broke it off. After a few more moments when it was clear the conversation was over the sergeant directed his work crew around the judge. They took a wide path, farther out than they had to.

"What was that about?" Rider asked Abbott from a few yards back.

Abbott watched as the soldiers awkwardly moved their load of boards around Stone and on down the street, "Got me, but I'm glad we're on this side of it."

The road through Alamosa led east and branched off a few dozen feet past the last building.

Both the main road and the branch road were dirt, but the branch road was new and was still muddy from all the recent rain. The main road drained well and was packed with both dirt and sand. This allowed it to drain easily during wet times but not lose its form during dry.

There was a steady flow of soldiers coming and going back and forth to the camp and the town. They were all in uniform and many were carrying tools or supplies. The Colorado militia uniform was a very dark color. It was hard to figure if it was more green or more black.

The sun was at its apex. There was mist in the air from all the water evaporating. It was getting humid. Making it feel hotter than it was. The humidity would not last long as the water burned off now with the full sun as the day slowly slipped into afternoon.

Stone dismounted his horse and took off his black duster. Rolling it up and putting it on the back of his saddle pack. He took his black vest off as well. Somehow through all the rain his black shirt underneath was bone dry and still looked pressed.

Abbott and Rider followed Stone's lead. Dismounting, stowing their heavier outer gear. Reorganizing things and getting their side arms out.

While everyone was getting situated Stone looked up at the Army camp which was up the branch road and up the hill at a few hundred feet higher elevation, "Jack, you remember what we did each morning back in the day?"

"Sure Judge, we did our formation and roll call," Abbott said, looking up at the camp with Stone.

"And why do military units do that each day?" Stone asked, not a question but leading Abbott with him as part of their agreement to try and be clearer with Abbott to Stone's thinking.

"To make sure everyone who was supposed to be there was, and everyone who was not supposed to be there was not," Abbott answered, from his training.

"You mean deserters?" Rider asked, following the conversation but not seeing where it was going. Her being a tough trail hand but having ever served in the military.

"Sure, deserters," Abbott answered, "but also anything else unauthorized too, like looting, gambling, general laziness, anything really you were not supposed to do, or that they wanted to catch you at, and to make sure if you were supposed to be off doing something you were" Abbott answered, turning to Stone. "You gonna ask Maddox to muster his entire regiment?"

"I was thinking about it. I am still trying to decide the best way to confront him about the unit he sent after us," Stone said, back to fiddling with his pack, "after a bit of discussion, of course. I do not know if I want a big show, but we need to figure out a way to get a count. See who is here and who ain't."

"You reckon the five-man unit was ordered after us by Maddox directly?" Rider asked.

"I do not see any other way around it. Whatever is going on here I just cannot comprehend how there can be too many people in on it at the top.

"You heard that soldier back there. Whatever else we might think of this Colorado outfit, they are acting like military. Soldiers get orders and follow them.

"Every soldier knows they are not to follow an illegal order. While it ain't always clear, I cannot imagine an awfully long chain of command where someone does not perk up and ask a question if given the order to hunt down a federal judge or go break someone out of jail," Stone said looking directly at Rider as he spoke since it was for her benefit.

"For McGuire, who was on trial for murder in a federal court," he continued, "they used red-shirts to do it. That is a closed members only post-war group. Not a group that is gonna do well in a chain of standard military command like all these fellas we see around here.

"Red-shirts are hold overs from the war. They been terrorizing for the past decade. Mostly in the south. Them being here suggests we are dealing with a very widespread event," Stone finished.

He thought for several more moments and seemed to come to a conclusion, "Ruth, I need you to keep on riding east to Fort Garland. It is only about a couple hours from here. Take these papers with you. There is a Major in charge there named Kenneth Borland. He got the same telegraph I did and will be expecting someone. He won't be expecting you, but I'll let your charisma and natural charms work all that out."

Rider looked at the papers, "You mind if I read them real quick Judge?" she asked, wanting to help but needing to know what she would be riding into.

Stone nodded to her and to the telegraph transcriptions he had handed her. All three stood quiet as Rider read the materials. She read them twice then after folding them back along their creases and putting them in her shirt top pocket, "Seems I am going to be the calvary," she smiled, "literally."

"Don't take too long," Stone said.

ALAMOSA

After Rider rode off Stone and Abbott walked their horses up the main road through Alamosa as it was being rebuilt. Having taken the fork up the new branch road to the military camp site they now stood in front of several militia guards who had sent word for what to do about them wanting to enter the camp. There was no nervousness in the soldiers. No impatience either.

They also were not bored as soldiers often are with guard duty.

"How long you fellas been in the Colorado militia?" Abbott asked while everyone was waiting around. Abbott had a way about him that made people comfortable. Certainly more than Stone who made people uncomfortable.

The youngest of the group was chatty and engaged in the conversation, "I signed up about four months ago sir," he said.

"Are you infantry?" Abbott asked, walking over to the young soldier, turning on his charisma.

"Yessir."

"I was infantry supply and logistics during the war," Abbott rolling a cigarette from the supplies he had bought at Wolf & Co. and offered one of his small flat rolling papers to the kid. Abbott actually did not smoke much. He knew this routine was an easy way to break the ice with a soldier. The kid took it and Abbott tapped a generous amount of tobacco onto the paper.

The other soldiers did not seem to think much of the exchange and went about being busy in place not really doing anything while everyone waited.

The kid knew what he was doing and quickly rolled the paper sealing it and produced a lit match in a long single move.

Abbott took a deep puff of his lit hand rolled cigarette and exhaled, "When I signed up, we didn't get much training. Things were moving quick. Now you boys get a couple weeks of training before they let you join your company," it was a good question but made as a statement. Simple and conversational but also set to collect some important information.

"Yessir. When I signed up, they only had the one training facility way out near Boulder. That is where I went. It was good training they were strict but spent a lot of time with us individually to make sure we got the basics down.

"But now they got training in Colorado City and another place in Glenwood Springs."

"Glenwood?" Abbott asked surprised, "there ain't a

whole lot of flat ground there."

"Yessir. That is apparently a special facility to mountain fighting. Ace high stuff."

Stone was listening without looking like we were listening. Abbott made a face of approval to show he thought the whole deal was ace high too.

A few more minutes passed and finally a small squad of four soldiers appeared. They talked quietly with the entry guards for a while then told Stone and Abbott that they were to leave their horses here and they would escort them to see the legal officer for the brigade, a Major Matt Kenny.

Two soldiers walk to the front and two to the rear of Stone and Abbott. It was all very friendly, but all the men showed good training. They were all fairly young as well. Stone and Abbott had yet to see any veterans that would be old enough to have also fought in the Civil War from a decade ago.

On the walk up the long slopping road Stone asked Abbott, "Jack, you got the list of registration numbers we pulled from those fella's gear?"

"Sure," Abbott said as they walked.

"Good," Stone said as his eyes sparkled in the late afternoon sun.

Just like any bureaucracy an infantry camp had layers of organization to it. It was divided into sections each of a particular type and serving a particular focus. This camp was no different.

Stone's initial impression of Maddox was that he was not

a very experienced military man. However, the camp here and the soldiers in general showed good design and good training. Stone was rarely wrong in his impressions, so he took it to mean there was some experienced military minds behind the Colorado militia other than Maddox. More support for the feeling that this whole thing was bigger than it appeared.

To the rear of the camp were maybe seven hundred tents grouped into rows of fifty across a quarter mile or so. If the enlisted were sharing tents one tent to two men, each row probably represented a company which was usually a hundred soldiers plus officers and other support.

In front of the tents were some larger tents. Administration, armory, supplies. In front of those some more permanent structures were being built. Larger buildings probably meant to house the command staff and general goings on. In front of those were yet more large tents. Most likely the temporary locations for the officers waiting on the permanent constructions to finish.

Stone and Abbott were walked to one set of the larger tents in front. A well-made sign said JAG Officer. There was a large desk outside the front of the tent under a flap to shade it from the sun. An impeccably dressed officer sat at the desk chair with his back to the tent opening. As they stopped in front of the desk Stone could see into the tent. There was a regulation cot made with military corners and some well stowed crisp looking uniforms.

Major Matt Kenny would be the legal officer for the brigade. As such, he was assigned to General Maddox as the legal officer for the Colorado militia but since the war no state or territory could have their own militia without officers who reported to federal departments. In this case the JAG officer worked for Maddox but reported to the Judge Advocate General in Washington DC. This made the local JAG officer independent of the local chain of command as his only source of orders.

It was convoluted on purpose. Many changes had been made to bring the country back together after the civil war. To have some level of controls in place to make sure succession never happened again. At least not through the military.

Abbott stayed back a few feet as the soldiers stopped and Stone approached the desk. He stood there for a few moments. Major Kenny continued writing onto a flat piece of white paper with a genuinely nice blue ink fountain pen.

Stone cleared his throat. The Major looked up briefly with a sign of irritation then back down to whatever he was writing.

Stone cleared his throat again, "Major Kenny," Stone said very friendly, "I know you are unaware at this moment, but military courtesy is to stand when presented with a higher-ranking member of your chain of command."

Kenny stopped his pen just for a second then continued writing, holding his left hand up to suggest he was almost done.

Stone waited patiently.

The sun was in the west. The afternoon was drawing on and the shadows getting longer. The first break from the heat could be felt on the edges of the calm mountain breeze.

After taking his good time Major Kenny folded up his papers and handed them to an enlisted soldier who took them and headed away from the tent.

Kenny then looked over to Judge Stone, "Judge, you're a civilian. I do not see how you have any authority here with the military. Even with an appointment as a special investigator," Kenny said looking past Stone to the four guards and giving them a head nod, which seemed to be for them to leave and return to whatever else they were supposed to be doing.

Stone looked at Kenny and spoke in is slow deep voice, "Major just so I do not get confused, where did you receive notification from that I would be wanting to talk to you?"

There was an edge to the question that Kenny caught, "General Maddox informed me," spoken with confidence.

"I see Major. My apologies. I was looking for the JAG officer of this here outfit not his staff. Would you please fetch him for me," Stone's voice carried a lot of nuance.

"No confusion I am the JAG officer," Kenny was still confident, but you could feel that confidence slipping at the edges.

"My understanding, major," Stone saying major in a way to suggest it was a subordinate rank, "is that a JAG officer in a territory or state militia, reports in through the Judge Advocate Generals office in Washington D.C. I seem to remember this being put into effect to avoid any confusion to a unit's loyalties. As a way to ensure, Jack what's that word President Grant said he wanted to ensure?"

Stone looked back over to Abbott.

This was an old drill. Abbott took a half step forward and said, "Yessir. Consistent strategic direction, sir," Abbott said very professionally to Stone.

Stone smiled and turned back to Kenny, "Consistent strategic direction," he repeated as though that provided a lot of insights to Kenny.

"Of course," Kenny said. An uncertain look crossed his face and he sat back down then stood back up quickly realizing that if Stone were correct, he may need to treat Stone as a superior.

As Major Kenny quickly stood back up Judge Stone casually sat down in one of the two chairs at the front of the desk opposite Kenny.

"Major, is there something," Stone trailed off looking at Kenny and prodding him to finish the statement.

"I'm going to need to confirm General Maddox's information to me sir," Kenny said, looking from Stone back to Abbott. "May I offer you my office here while I head to our communications company," Kenny extending an arm to indicate the large tent behind him.

Stone studied Kenny, but otherwise remained silent, and seated.

Kenny slowly stood to attention and then walk off east towards another one of the larger administrative areas. Stone could see telegraph wires leading into the tent in front of the unfinished building and assumed several telegraphs were about to be sent and received.

Stone and Abbott were now by themselves outside

the Major's tent. There were other military folks here and there about the general area. None, however, close enough to be engaged in a conversation.

A breeze was picking up from the north and there was the start of rain clouds in the sky. Nothing definite but more than a few hours ago. From the slightly higher elevation of the army camp, you could see back over the town very easily. If you were expecting trouble from the west or south this camp location was very strategic.

The Ute Indian Reservation was not more than sixty miles west and south of Alamosa. The San Juan mountain range separated the two locations.

Both Stone and Abbott were looking over the town and marveling at the natural beauty of the place. From their vantage point if they looked south there were lakes bluer than the sky, north green flowered pastures giving way to yellow and brown desert, east white mountain peaks.

"Jack," Stone looked from the scenic views over to Abbott who returned the look, "when Kenny gets back, I want you to stay here with him and research those serial numbers. After that, no matter what you find I want you to ride over to Fort Garland too. Meet up with Ruth there."

Abbott quickly objected, "Judge I aim to see this through with you," he said working up other objections but Stone interceded.

"No Jack. I know you have my back and I know you would follow me anywhere. But our work here is almost done. What I said in Poole's house do not carry no weight. The law is what is needed not some angry old has-beens trying to bring justice. I ain't no avenger and neither are you. It is a new day and we need to play within the new rules.

"You get the evidence and then get yourself over to the federal fort. I still plan on talking to Maddox, then I will meet you there tomorrow. "

Abbott studied Stone for a few moments, "Judge I'll go with you to talk to Maddox then we'll both ride over to Fort Garland together tonight. Makes more sense. Besides that way if something goes wrong there will be two of us. Just in case."

Stone smiled, "Ain't gonna be no shootout Jack we're in this man's camp and he is the General not us. I would rather know you are gone and with the evidence we need. That way even if he does try and detain me you will be able to get the word out and come back and get me with an appropriate cadre of help.

"This ain't the trip neither of us thought we were on. You need to get home to your wife and kids. I know you miss them I can see it on you. And they miss you. You will be more help to me loaded with real legal evidence and out from underneath the thumb of this militia anyway."

"I do not like it Judge."

"We all got to do things we don't like from time-to-time Jack. You know that as much as I do. More probably being a father and husband. And businessman."

Kenny returned before Abbott could raise another objection. He had two enlisted men with him and he looked mad and uncomfortable, "The General isn't going to like you investigating him and crawling through his armory records," he saluted Stone when he returned but there was no respect in it.

"Major, Jack here and I were just talking about that some-times you got to do things you ain't all that crazy about," Stone said looking from Kenny to Abbott.

Abbott showed a small amount of frustration but also some relief that Stone's orders had been confirmed and that Kenny was willing to fulfill his role as the JAG officer, "The General is currently under investigation for issuing unlawful orders," Abbott said to Kenny taking the lead from Stone per his earlier request, "it wouldn't surprise me at all that he isn't going to like that one bit."

Kenny thought for a moment and reread the papers he had returned with. He looked from Abbott to Stone, "Do you honestly believe General Maddox ordered men from this regiment to hunt you down and try and murder you? Or that he, we, had anything to do with the massacre at Alamosa?"

Abbott answered again establishing for Kenny that he was now on point for this, "Major, we can both get a simple answer to that right now if we walk over to the armory and take a look at the registration numbers for a couple of your rifles," Abbotts voice was serious. Not like Stone's but there was enough of an edge to it that sug-gested Kenny should do as Abbott suggested.

"Major," Stone said to Kenny as Abbott started to shuffle him off to the armory tent, "which one of these tents does Maddox use?"

Kenny looked at Stone for an exceedingly long time before answering, weighing something, "The General is currently inspecting the new construction down in Alamosa. Then I believe he is headed to meet up with one of our other regiments west of here. But there should be time to catch him. He is a stickler for a good inspection, making sure the town is being rebuilt to the highest standards."

Stone looked over to Abbott, "Jack you finish up here then head out like we discussed. I will go talk to General Maddox," Stone started the long walk down the hill to where his horse was waiting.

Abbott followed Major Kenny up past the command tents eventually reaching a small set of tents just outside the main thoroughfare. They walked in where a smartly dressed Sergeant was seated in front of a table. Behind him were rows of well-organized ammunition and firearms. To his left were several large wood cabinets. Kenny asked the Sergeant for the registration papers for field riffles that included dates purchased and serial numbers.

The sergeant, after snapping to attention and giving a few 'yessirs' spent several minutes going through large sets of paper. Abbott noted, having run supply himself during the war that, just as before, the Colorado regiment took its job seriously and the soldiers seemed to take soldiering seriously as well. Things were very military and crisp. Organized.

Kenny had a slow look of recognition cross his face while he and Abbott were waiting, "Abbott Horse Farms?"

Abbott smiled a little and got humble, "Yep. Rounded up a good number of Morgan Colts after the war in Maryland and drove them out here to Colorado. They were a good base. Good horses."

Kenny's entire demeanor changed, he reached out to shake Abbotts hand, "Wow I did not realize. It is a pleasure to meet you! The stories about the quality of your horses and your ability to turn even the weakest colt into a fine mount are well known."

"Horses do all the work. I just encourage them a little. Sometimes point them in the right direction. My two boys have mostly taken over the business. They got the knack even better than me. I could not be prouder of them," Abbott had a pleasant look cross his face thinking about his family and the life he was able to create for them after he war.

Kenny smiled also and looked at Abbott maybe a bit longer than he needed to. A sad look quickly crossed his face and he started to say something else when the desk sergeant produced the requested paperwork.

The segreant saluted Kenny as he handed over several papers, "These are all checked out to a single squad sir. Reporting to Lieutenant Paul Malborne of the fifth."

Kenny reviewed the match himself then said to Abbott, "This is a special unit. A kill squad. We only have four of them in a single company. I actually did question the General when he created them. I didn't see any need," Kenny clearly wanted Abbott to believe he was caught unaware concerning this information.

A military special unit was a unit that had unique capabilities and could take on missions that require technical skills or knowledge beyond regular soldering. There were many types of special units, not all orientated to combat or hostilities. There were special medical units. Special construction units that could build bridges and other earthworks. The JAG office Kenny was attached to was a special legal unit.

During the civil war, a kill squad was usually a group of questionable characters whose mission was to go behind enemy lines and cause general chaos. Or they would be given specific targets to harass or eliminate. They were given an objective but allowed to go about the work in their own way. Often because it would be done counter to any legal orders that could be given. And often because the men in these units did not do well with direct orders anyway.

Abbott looked solemnly at Kenny. "Can I assume Major that the five men in this squad are not here in camp. Could you produce them?" Abbott said to Kenny as they stood inside the armorer's tent.

Kenny went through the process of going over the paperwork again. Abbott got the feeling he might be buying time or trying to make a decision. Kenny was starting to perspire.

"Fifth company is our kill company," Kenny said, not making eye contact. "They are all highly trained. When I talked to General Maddox about the need for them, he explained that we might need to harass the Indians if hostilities returned. I did not think it made sense at the time, but I also did not think too much about it at all really. It is not wildly out of place for us to have these units."

Kenny was now visibly sweating, and he looked rather pale.

It was getting late in the afternoon and there were probably only two or three hours of daylight left. The wind had picked up some and it was threatening to start raining again. A quick turn from the niceness of earlier in the day. A thunder rolled through the camp so huge and loud it shook the earth.

Abbott and Kenny were walking back to Kenny's tent when Kenny offered, "Lt. Malborne and his squad are currently on assignment and not present in the camp."

"We are going to need your help Major," Abbott returned. "we have ourselves a problem here. Our fear is that it's a much larger problem than just one missing squad."

Kenny thought for a few seconds, "You got yourself a problem not me. All I hear is speculation and a few coincidences."

Abbott was surprised at the turn. He had not expected it. As Stone had explained to him the entire point of the JAG role in these post war outfits was to be the eyes and ears for the federal government to make sure states kept their focus on the nation and not individual exploits.

Abbott looked Kenny in the eye, "Think hard Major. This is all gonna clear out. You do not want to be on the wrong side of it. Not if you're a career man like I think you are."

"I see it. But that does not mean nothing. You get me something official from my chain of command, from Washington, and I'm your man," Kenny said, it seemed he was being honest. "I understand Judge Stone has a special role to play, but that is murky. I cannot go up against the General unless I get something specific. After the federal authorities in the War Department know our findings.

Something that is more tangible. You come at me side-ways," Kenny continued, "or try and position me on a different side from General Maddox with only telegraph papers. I'm not gonna be overly helpful."

Kenny continued after some more internal deliberation, "Let's you and I go down and talk to General Maddox and Judge Stone in town now. Let's get everything out in the open. I need to report back to General Maddox about what I found anyway. He is a good man. A good solider. He has an extremely specific vision for this unit. He will not be any more pleased to hear that some men under his command may have gone rogue than you were. I think we are all on the same side of things."

Abbott watched Kenny hurry down the path towards town. He was not thrilled about the turn in Kenny, but he followed him not seeing a lot of other options.

MAGGIE SUMMERS

A s Stone walked away from Abbott and Kenny, he could see all the way into town from the elevation in the landscape he was on. Down in town a grouping of soldiers were following someone around. This was probably Maddox and his staff starting their building inspections.

It would take Stone about twenty minutes to make his way down the road and into town.

Stone felt an expected change in the air and on queue Maggie spoke to him, "Judge I know what happens next. But I ain't never seen it like this neither.

"Something changed but I do not know what.

"Before I could have gone back and looked or gone forward and seen the now from a different angle. A different perspective.

"But being bound here all I can do now is see you.

"I fear this is not the right way. Time is not moving in the right direction.

"Yet you keep slowly moving forward towards it and all I

can do is follow."

Stone was fed up with Maggie. He was fed up with the whole situation. As was typical this spirit was going to get him angry which could mean him missing something or acting out of anger rather than logic.

If this were the end of Maggie's journey Stone felt it was time to clear the air, "Maggie, you told me once you were telling things straight. Is that still true?" he said as he walked down the highlands road.

There had been storm clouds in the distance and they still hung around the edges of things threatening rain later in the day. He could see them on the horizon to the west and north. The south and east had mountains covering the horizon so they could be all around. He would have no way to know.

Maggie's voice became soft and small in his head, "Yes I always told you straight."

"Then we have a problem don't we Maggie."

"Judge, I did not know if you heard me near the other rider. There was a lot going on. But you knew anyway. You were just waiting for me to say it."

"I knew it from the beginning, Maggie. McGuire told the truth in everything. So did Burton. You brought charges against a person in my court falsely. You lied under oath. You murdered William, your husband."

Thunder suddenly rumbled through the valley loud. It came in hard and shook the ground. The sky was still blue but the storms around the edges were getting larger. More pronounced in their dark clouds.

Stone continued, "You wanted to sell out to McGuire. You wanted the money. I am sure it was a lot. More than your land was worth. Then William said no. That he wanted to make a life. Have a family. Build something.

"You resented it.

"You resented him.

"You were not trying to buy time like you said. You wanted your youth back. You felt it was wasted now and for nothing. You blamed William and everyone else but yourself.

"You wanted time to go backwards so you could start over. Make better decisions. Be young again.

"You told me that but not straight like you said."

Stone nodded to the camp guards as he walked past and collected his horse leaving Abbott's mount in place. It was getting cold so he removed his black duster and put it on, tying the back near the waste around so his two side arms would be easy to use.

He slowly walked the horse down the path, "I saw the look too," when he was out of earshot of the soldiers, remembering the exchange between Maggie and McGuire when she was on the stand, "I saw that you and McGuire were in cahoots. You had practiced your little show in court.

"McGuire told you about magic ways. Ancient arts. Tempting you with unnatural dealings. You wanted to go back in time and sure enough he delivered on that promise using darkness. It is never what you think it is but always what was agreed.

"Marks was in on it too. Lord knows what deal he made.

"On the stand when you got nervous, he helped you with a line.

"Motive.

"I remember Maggie. That was not my first day in court.

"The shadows were everywhere. You could not see them then, but you can see them now. They love the little lies. The little parts that make it not the truth when enough of it is to change the meaning. They feed on it. Like you said they drink it like water and breathe it like air. It sustains them and they gorged themselves that day and night.

"You thought you were playing me but the whole time the shadows were playing you.

"Now they own you.

"Justice ain't what you think it is Maggie. It rarely is anyway but you made it worse.

"Justice does not start with your hanging by the redshirts down there in Alamosa. It starts with you murdering your husband as a sacrifice to get something you desperately wanted. Probably before that even.

"I am about to bring you justice just like you said. Just like you thought you wanted when you were playing me.

"I am about to bring justice down on this valley like no one has ever seen. Not even you in all your travels. You have never seen this moment before because it has never happened before.

"It can't happen even now. I agreed. We all agreed. But I

keep my word. Even when it goes against the agreement that I offered it for. Just like you did.

"Maggie, you tell them when they come for you that I am bringing justice to Alamosa. And I am bringing you with me to deliver it."

GUS MADDOX

Geneial Maddox and six of his direct reports were walking from building to building in town. Several of the soldiers with him were writing down on paper things he said as he pointed here and there. At each of the buildings it appeared the work crew responsible for the rebuild was waiting. Each crew ready for the inspection of them and their work so far.

Alamosa looked nothing like it did before. The new construction was not simply replacing the old construction. It must have taken a week or more to clear away the original buildings and debris. Or at least what was left of them. There were many foundations that were being rebuilt and several other foundations that had been cleared so they could be used later.

The new layout was very orderly. It was not immediately apparent what each of the new buildings would be. It was clear however that they would all be about the same size and have the same facings.

"Looks like you're rebuilding the town General," Stone said conversationally and loudly as he tied his horse to a hitch post near the current building Maddox was inspecting.

Maddox and his entourage all seemed surprised at the new voice. They stopped their conversation to turn and look at Stone who waved at Maddox very friendly.

There was a moment of confusion for Maddox and his group. Not worry, just calm uncertainty. A black clad white bearded man carrying two pistols in his belt simply did not register with them.

After just a moment recognition crossed Maddox's face and he fully turned to face Stone, "Judge Sir, if you would do me the honor of explaining why you are here, and what it is that I can help you with, I will expedite it immediately for you so you may be on your way," Maddox said, sounding confident and powerful as he started to walk to Stone, his men stepping out of his way.

Both men held eye contact and the wind picked up. The storm clouds were now clearly visible but not yet fully formed or over the town. The sun still shown. It was a bright afternoon with a lot of dark edges.

The scene was picturesque.

The light from the sun was very bright. Highlighted by its intensity and the dust in the windy air causing rays to be visible here and there. The wind swept hard and the dark clouds held their ground. Not advancing on the town and not retreating.

Maddox stood facing the light almost glowing at the edges. His hand on his sword hilt and looking very much like a military General. Maddox could sense Stone was different this time. That he had his own aura of authority. A dangerous man.

They stood now facing each other just a few yards apart. Maddox's staff had formed a half circle to either side of him.

The scene was very much of one against many.

Stone could see both up and down the main street in Alamosa with Maddox and his group on the side of the road with the military camp up in the background behind them. He could see two figures coming down the highlands trail from the camp. It looked like Abbott and Kenny.

Maddox finally spoke again to Stone, "You here as a Judge or something else?"

Stone smiled and looked back at Maddox, "Gus that's a solid question. It shows good insights by you."

Stone was being soft spoken now, but the edge was still there. With military, using their first name was a sign of intimacy, or disrespect, depending. Intimacy if you were of a higher rank and talking to a subordinate, to show you valued them as a person. Disrespect if you were talking to a superior, disregarding their rank as compared to yours. Maddox made a very disapproving face as did a few of his men. None of them quite sure which situation applied.

"You can address me as General, or sir, or if you like General sir," Maddox said to Stone in a commanding voice.

Stone ignored the suggestion, "Gus, I'm investigating some men from your unit. Means I'm also investigating you," Stone looked from Maddox to the men around him, "and I suppose you fellas as well," somehow his soft tone carried more command than Maddox's loud voice.

"For you," Maddox began trying to regain a sense of being in charge. Of telling people what's what, "things are black and white, right and wrong, good and bad."

"I'd say that's how it is for most folks," Stone interrupted. He knew this was not really a conversation. He also knew Maddox had decided to put a show on for his men and interrupting him would frustrate that.

Maddox continued, "You think that when a person does something good, they are right. When they do something bad, they are wrong," showing force when he spoke.

He was in his own head now. Not listening to anything but his own thoughts, "But that's not the correct view of things. See, I learned through years of watching people suffer, sometimes at my own hand, that the world isn't made that way."

His men smiled at the idea of people suffering at Maddox's hand. They clearly saw him as their leader and a dominant person both physically and mentally, "It's all about power," Maddox's eyes brightened, and his voice became even louder.

"If I have power then whatever I do is good. Being powerful, I decide what is good. I decide what is bad.

"I tried to explain this to you once before. You were unable to listen right. To understand.

"That's why your world view is wrong. People do not sometimes do good and sometimes do bad. The world ain't a court of law.

"This is why men like you fail," Maddox was working himself and his men into something, "It's not about what someone does. It is about how much power they have when they do it."

Stone held eye contact with Maddox, who's eyes were wide with excitement, "It's not about good and bad General, it's about good and evil," he said back. While his voice did not have volume, it had bass. It made it seem that Maddox had lost the argument. It undid his confident assertions.

Stone knew Maddox would not listen but continued, "the truth is, what an evil man does will always be evil, it ain't objective or subjective," Stone could now see clearly that Major Kenny was walking up main street towards the group and that Abbott was very close behind him.

Maddox cut him off after his last statement. Not having time for another viewpoint or interested in any kind of conversation. He was engaged and excited and responded to Stone's comment with an energetic "No!"

Maddox now was yelling, "There is no objective truth. There is only the perspective of the powerful.

"We decide what is good.

"Our founders claim to pursue happiness.

"Happiness is not a pursuit! It is a consequence!

"A consequence and direct measure of power.

"Judge you claim to pursue justice. To right a wrong. Change what people believe about things. To be here to do something.

"But powerful men already decided.

"They did not ask you because you carry no weight.

"There ain't nothing you are going to do that is gonna change anything. Your only choice now is how much interest do you want us to take of you when this is over."

Kenny and Abbott were now within earshot of the group. Maddox paused looking down the street to Kenny. For his part, Stone's expression had not changed. If anything, he looked even more calm in his opposition to Maddox.

"It's interesting Gus, you and me," Stone began and was interrupted by Kenny.

"General sir," Kenny approached and saluted Maddox, "we have discovered some information about the fifth that you need to be alerted to."

Something clicked with Maddox. He lost interest in Stone. His demeanor changed, "Okay Major calm down. Judge if you will excuse us please. I apparently need to hear the Majors report."

With that Maddox, Kenny and the rest of the group walked several yards away out of earshot. Kenny was explaining something to Maddox. He was very animated in his explanation.

"Jack I specifically asked you to get the information and head out," Stone said to Abbott.

Stone was mad with Abbott for not doing as he had requested.

"It did not work out that way Judge. The Major there changed his tune and made a bee line for down here."

Stone made an angry face at Abbott and looked back to

the group of soldiers.

Maddox and his crew talked together for a few more minutes. After a short while it seemed a decision had been made. Maddox gestured for Stone, "Judge would you come over here please. This is new information; it changes some of what I thought we were talking about."

Stone exchanged a wary glance with Abbott and started to cross the twenty or so yards between him and Maddox's group. Major Kenny was walking back and the two crossed in between. Kenny nodding to Stone and giving a wink as if to say things had been cleared up as they passed.

Abbott started to slowly follow Stone so he could stand apart but still hear what was being said. Kenny stopped near Abbott and stood just behind him as Stone reached the group.

Maddox made a welcoming gesture for Stone to come even closer as if inviting him into his inner circle. The six men near Maddox stepped away a little to make room for Stone who stopped short of the group. Maddox also stepped slightly to the side.

Suddenly there was a commotion behind Stone. As he turned, he heard Abbott yell "Judge look," which was immediately cut off by the report of a pistol. Kenny had attempted to shoot Stone in the back. Abbott had seen it and acted quickly jumping in the way.

Abbott fell to the ground and was motionless. A large hole in him. The round passing from front to back at close range through his chest being hugely destructive

Two of Maddox's men were on Stone before he could

react. Blood and bone sprayed out of Abbott and covered Stone hitting him in the face and covering him in Abbotts blood.

Stone dropped to his knees as the two men held him. He was in shock and working to understand what was happening. Everything started happening in slow motion. He saw Maddox walk over to Abbotts body and give it a kick. There was no life left.

Maddox slowly wiped his shoe to get the blood off on a part of Abbotts shirt, "Power," he started to say.

Stone stared at the scene working to recover. Anger growing in him. Coming up from a depth that was very deep and very primal.

Stone was in no mood for any more speeches. He was furious with rage and started to yell. It was not a word but just a noise of both grief and anger. Maddox watched with a look of smug curiosity on his face as his men held firm.

The yell grew louder. The wind picked up. Lightning struck several times nearby. The air filled with thunder.

Maggie appeared near Stone. A ghostly spirit apparition of horror. She appeared screaming just as Stone was. In the same position on the ground next to him. Adding an otherworldly wail to Stone's primal call.

Maddox's look of curiosity slowly fell into a look of confusion.

Maggie looked up at the men holding Stone. Her hair was full of static electricity. Her eyes glowed bright yellow. Her neck was too long and her jaw to wide as it mirrored the sorrow in her terrifying scream. She was covered red in blood and the front of her neck was ripped out still carrying the noose on it that had been her earthly demise.

But she was real.

The slowness of time snapped. Things started happening fast.

Moving at an unnatural speed she bounded between the two men holding Stone. The light from their eyes faded as she used her long fingers as claws and scratched and ripped at them. An ethereal attack that seemed to rip the spirit from their body leaving it lifeless.

Stone let his yell fad watching Maggie. He felt a small sense of relief that she had understood their last conversation and he would be able to reprieve her from the eternity of torment she almost had to endure.

Maddox's expression had changed from confusion to one of concern as he watch the ghast that Maggie had become move from man to man. Ending the life of his soldiers with little effort.

It would take Stone a long time to recover from the death of his friend, but he was no stranger to loss and knew how to focus in the moment to finish what needed finishing. He put his hands on his knees and pushed himself to a standing position focusing on Maddox.

Maddox was bewildered as Maggie bounded from man to man until the last of his staff fell. She then slowly walked over to stand besides Stone.

She stood next to him. Clearly his ally.

The three figures were in the middle of a cyclone that obscured everything else. The town, the valley, the mountain range, none of it was visible just a wall of wind and the local scene of carnage.

Maggie looked at Maddox and hissed, "You sent McGuire to take our land. You sent the men who killed me."

Maddox covered his ears as his expression fell to horror then became even more intense.

Slowly stepping in Maddox's direction, she continued, "You ruined everything. I never would have done what I done if not for you. Then afterwards we had a deal! But you did not honor your words. You sent men to kill me! Do you know what they did to me! Do you have any idea what it is like to die slow up there on a rope?"

"Maggie," Stone spoke soft, comforting.

Maggie turned back to Stone. Not a threatening gesture. Like a child that wants to go run and play but needs her parent's permission and was not sure she would get it. She stopped and waited for Stone to speak again.

"This gonna be all of it then?" he asked her.

"Yes," she said. In Stone's eyes she changed back to how he remembered her from before the trial. It was clear to Maddox, she remained the terrifying entity.

"This next bit is really important. Take your time before you answer as I am judging you now. You must know why it is okay to finish this. You must tell me now. I cannot be the one to tell you. I have to hear you speak it," he said with a small gesture.

Maggie looked over to Maddox and back to Stone, "I know why Judge. Because my story with you does not start with me killing William. It starts when these men decided they wanted my land. When they sent McGuire in with his black magic to tempt me. Because even though I was weak and I deserved what came, that did not bring justice."

She looked directly at him, "But we both know that this will. Like you said, justice depends on where you start the story. You have taught me that it also depends on where you end it."

Stone made a face of resolution and nodded, "You are free like you wanted but you don't have long. Do what you need to do. I will make sure justice follows you."

Maggie turned and raced to Maddox screaming rage as an avenging angel might. Maddox screamed in a high pitch and fell to his knees, moving his hands from his ears to his face just as she enveloped him. The light around him faded and he fell. Gone.

As Maddox died thunder rolled through the valley again. Thick loud rumbling thunder that did not sound natural. It almost sounded like a horn.

From all the edges the small shadows started to emerge.

Dancing around in anticipation. Expecting to feast on the beaten soul of a tragedy.

As the thunder cleared, they slowly started to move forward. Around from all sides. Picking up speed until they were moving quickly. Running to Maggie with the intent to consume her.

Maggie had no fear. She watched them as they grew closer. When they were almost on her she looked over to Stone who nodded his goodbye.

Sunlight broke the clouds and shown on her.

Maggie faded away with a content look on her face just before the shadows reached her. In that moment, the storm ended. The wind stopped and things returned to normal.

Dusk had fallen and there was still some sunlight making its way over the western mountains illuminating the valley.

Stone fell to his knees and cradled Abbott. The other soldiers in the town slowly started to emerge from the structures and were looking at the dead bodies of their fallen commanders. Trying to understand what had happened.

Stone was aware that Ruth and a large number of Cavalry from Fort Garland had entered the head of the road from the south and were making their way up to the main part of town.

Stone's eyes teared up. He would not cry, but he was sad. He had miscalculated from the start what he was dealing with in Maddox and many had died because of it. Including his good friend Jack Abbott.

Stone now understood that there was something much larger going on. Something that threatened everyone in the territory and possibly more. Maddox had been the lead to part of it, but he was not the head man. There were clearly evil forces at work that needed stopping.

A breeze picked up. The air changed. Dread filled Stone. Ice went down his spine and he wanted to be anywhere but here in Alamosa.

He felt drawn away. It was a yearning. A desperate excuse to leave this hard luck crossroads town for any reason he could invent.

When he looked up into the mountains or looked over to the bright blue lake or looked north to the green flowered pastures, he wanted to go there instead of staying here.

He feared to his core and deep in his soul what he would hear next.

He wondered for the first time ever if the deal was worth it.

Stone released Abbotts body and forced his head up, "Thank you for saving my life Jack," Stone said to the air behind him.

The End.

Made in the USA
Columbia, SC
11 March 2021

34309156R00114